WHEN THE STARS
BEGIN TO FALL

JAMES LINCOLN COLLIER

When the Stars Begin to Fall

dp *Delacorte Press/New York*

Published by
Delacorte Press
1 Dag Hammarskjold Plaza
New York, N.Y. 10017

Manufactured in the United States of America

First printing

Library of Congress Cataloging in Publication Data

Collier, James Lincoln, [date of birth]
  When the stars begin to fall.

  Summary: Angry and frustrated that his entire family is considered to be poor trash, fourteen-year-old Harry defies his father and attempts to prove that a factory is polluting their small Adirondack community.
  [1. Pollution—Fiction. 2. Adirondack Mountains (N.Y.)—Fiction. 3. Poverty—Fiction. 4. Fathers and sons—Fiction] I. Title.
PZ7.C678We 1986   [Fic]
ISBN 0-385-29516-2
Library of Congress Catalog Card Number: 86-11619

For Asa

ONE

I was up in my room trying to fix my stereo when I heard the car drive in. I looked out the window. An old Buick was coming up the dirt driveway, going slow so as not to splash water up out of the puddles in the drive left over from last night's rain. I couldn't see who was in the car, but I knew it was Charlie Fritz and some friend of his. I knew what they were coming for too. They were going to get my sister, Helen, up in the barn with them. That's all they ever came around for. I hated it when they came. It made me feel rotten, and usually when it happened I would go out for a walk.

I decided to concentrate on getting my stereo to work right. It wasn't much of a record player. Dad had found it in the town dump and brought it home for me. It had a bad hum. I'd figured I could fix it, but I never had been able to get the hum out, so it wasn't much use to me. Still, I kept trying.

I heard the doors to the Buick slam, and then I

heard them knock on the kitchen door. The front door was nailed shut because it was so warped that if you opened it you'd never get it shut again. I heard Helen let them in, and then I could hear them talking and laughing. I figured they'd brought some beer. They usually did when they came to see Helen.

I wished Mom were home. When Mom was home, they took Helen off for a drive in the Buick, and I didn't have to know anything about it. But Mom had walked down the road to Mrs. O'Brien's to watch one of her shows there, because our TV didn't get that channel too clearly. I didn't know where Dad was. He never told us where he was going. He just got up in the morning, hardly said anything to anyone, ate his breakfast, and got into the truck and went. Sometimes Mom would say, "Frank, where will you be in case anybody wants to know?" He wouldn't even answer. He'd just grunt and go out and drive away, and not come back until supper time.

So my sister was safe for a while. She was sixteen, I was fourteen. I didn't want to think about it, so I made myself concentrate on the stereo. After a little while I heard the kitchen door open and shut, and their voices outside. They were going up to the barn. I decided to get out of the house. I couldn't get that stereo to work anyway.

I waited until they had got into the barn and were out of sight, and then I went downstairs and out through the kitchen door. It was almost the end of April but still cool, and the grass didn't need to be cut yet. Dad said he didn't care if it was ever cut—that was too tidy and middle-class for him; he didn't care if it grew up into a hay field. But I kept it cut—as much as I could anyway—with our old mower. It helped the looks of the old place some, but there wasn't much you could do about dressing it up. The paint was mostly peeled off, and some of the window-panes were missing and Dad had filled them in with cardboard. The old gardens that had once been there were full of weeds, and big rocks sat on top of the garbage cans out back so the raccoons wouldn't knock the tops off and spread the garbage all over the yard. Dad always said he didn't care if the place fell down; it wasn't his, why should he put time and money into somebody else's place? That made sense, but still I wished we had a place like most of the kids around there had, with nice lawns and curtains in the windows and rugs and things. We didn't have much furniture, and it all came from secondhand stores. The sofa had a hole that Mom kept a towel over, and there was nothing on the living room floor but a little old beat-up hooked rug. Dad always said he couldn't afford any better, and besides, he didn't want all that middle-class nonsense anyway.

Besides, there was always a couple of junkers sitting next to the driveway that Dad had bought for a few bucks and towed home with the idea of repairing and selling them for a few hundred. He would do it, too—he was kind of a junk expert and could generally figure out a way to get some value out of things somebody else had thrown away. But usually it took him months to get around to it, and meanwhile the junkers would sit there with their tires flat and the bodies rusting and weeds growing up around them.

There wasn't much hope of dressing the place up, but I cut the lawn anyway. It helped some. Mom liked it when I did it. She always said I was the only one who ever did anything around there.

I went across the lawn feeling sad and low about everything—the weeds in the garden and the paint peeling off the house, and Helen up there in the barn with Charlie Fritz and that other guy. I crossed the lawn, and jumped over the stone wall that divided the old pasture from the lawn. Sumac and small cedars were beginning to grow in the pasture. In a few years it would be filled with brush, and after that the woods would come down the hillside and take over. I trotted up the sloping pasture to the woods beyond the next stone wall. I liked going into the woods. They were clean and natural, and there wasn't anything junky there. I climbed over the stone wall and stood there looking around. Being so far upstate New York, the trees were just beginning to bud, and when you looked off through the woods, it was like a thin yellow light was coming out of them. I looked down. There was a patch of moss right where I was standing. I knelt and ran my hand over it to feel the softness, carefully, so as not to tear any of it up.

Then I sat down on the stone wall, and began looking through the woods for birds. I knew about birds. I'd been studying them for years. I loved seeing them swoop and dart. They moved so fast, you could hardly believe it. You'd see one take off, and the next thing it'd be all the way over to the other side of the pasture. That time of year there was always plenty of birds around—dark-eyed juncos, tufted titmice, nuthatches, and lots more. The nuthatches made me laugh, because they walked up tree trunks upside down.

I was interested in fish too. Sometimes I would go down to some creeks and streams I knew about, and lie by the bank watching the fish down in the water. You couldn't do that on the Timber River, which was the big one around there, because it was polluted, but you could on the little streams that fed into it. It was terrible the way the Timber River had got polluted, but nobody seemed to be able to do anything about it.

So I sat there on the stone wall watching the birds. I wished I had a pair of binoculars. Old Man Greenberg sold them in the Sports Center. The ones I wanted cost forty dollars, and I never could get forty dollars together. Every time I got fifteen or twenty dollars saved, something would come along that I had to pay for—new tires for my bike, or a school trip or something. It was no use asking Dad for stuff like that. He always said he was broke, and besides, he wasn't about to spend a lot of money on stuff like that.

After a while I heard voices, and I knew they were coming down out of the barn. I went back across the pasture. I could see the three of them come out of the barn and head for the car. I climbed over the stone wall into the yard. Charlie Fritz and the other guy got into the car. Helen stood there near the car. She was frowning and looking sad. "Where are you guys going?" she said.

"No place special," they said.

Her shoulders sagged, but she didn't dare ask if she

could go with them, because she was afraid they would say no. So she stood there watching until they had driven away. She looked sad and frowned. Then she saw me come across the lawn. "What are you looking at?" she said crossly.

"Are you in love with Charlie Fritz?" I said.

"What makes you think that?" she said.

"It seemed like it," I said. "You shouldn't go up to the barn with those guys. If Dad ever catches you, he'll kill you."

"I don't care," she said. "It's none of his business."

Then she went into the house and up to her room. I knew she felt lousy because those guys hadn't asked her to come with them. They never did. And the reason why they never did was because we were trash. Some people said we were no-goods. Some said we were low. But mostly they said we were trash. Mom was trash, and Dad was trash, and my sister and I were trash. Nobody in town would have anything to do with us if they could help it. It took me quite a while to learn this. But things slowly happened, and I learned it.

The first thing that happened was when I was little, five or six. Maybe even littler than that. Helen and I were playing somewhere. All I can remember is that it was a grassy place and we were playing with a bunch of kids. Some woman came along in a station wagon and said for everybody to get in, she would take the kids for a Carvel. But when Helen and I started to get in, she said we couldn't come with the other kids. She said she couldn't have us in her car. When we got home later, we told Mom. She put her head down on the kitchen table and cried. Helen and I didn't understand it, and we forgot about it. Years later I remembered it, and I realized why the woman wouldn't let us get in her car. It was because we had cooties in our hair.

By the time I was in the second grade, I was beginning to see that the other kids didn't like us. When we tried to go over and play with them in school, they would usually say, "You stink." I never thought much of it. I figured it was just the kind of thing kids would say to each other.

But then one day when I was in the third grade, I walked into the classroom and somebody had written on the blackboard "Harry White stinks." Suddenly I knew they meant it.

I got red and felt uncomfortable and sat in my seat looking down at my desk. Then I began to lose my temper, the way I always do. I stood up and shouted out, "I'll punch the one who did that." They all started to shout back, "You stink, Harry, you stink." Just then Mrs. McGarvey came in and they shut up. She erased the words from the blackboard and said that she would keep everybody after if it happened again. Then, when three o'clock came, she kept me after and talked to me.

"Harry, do you have a bathtub in your house?" she said.

"Sure," I said, trying to figure out why she was asking that.

"And a washing machine for clothes?"

"No," I said. "We don't have a washing machine."

"How does your mom wash your clothes?" she said.

I stood there thinking, and after a minute my head got hot and I scratched my scalp. I couldn't remember how she washed our clothes. "I guess she does it some way," I said.

"Harry," Mrs. McGarvey said, "I think the other children would be nicer to you if you took a bath every day. And ask your mom to be more frequent about washing your clothes."

I couldn't wait to get out of there, I was blushing so hot. It was true. We stank. We weren't clean. I stank and my sister, Helen, stank too.

I felt red and sweaty, and I didn't dare take the school bus home but walked the whole four miles up to Mountain Pass Road, where we lived. I didn't say anything to Mom or Dad but went right into Helen's room to tell her about it.

Our rooms were pretty small, but it didn't matter because we didn't have much furniture anyway—just our beds and a table for doing our homework on, and hooks that we'd put up for our clothes. We kept some of our clothes in the cardboard boxes under our beds.

Helen was lying on her bed when I came in; she was wearing her old blue jeans and an old sweater. I looked at her and I saw that Mrs. McGarvey was right. There was a big cocoa stain on the front of her sweater, the knees of her blue jeans were dirty, and one of them had a hole as big as a quarter. There was dirt in her fingernails, dirt on her hands, dirt around her ankles where they came out of her socks. "Helen, we stink," I said. And I told her what had happened at school.

She jumped off the bed and started for me. "It isn't true," she shouted. "It's a lie." She started to swing at me.

I jumped out of the way. "Don't hit me," I said. "I didn't say it."

"I'll get them," she shouted. "I'll get the ones who said it."

But after that she was in the bathroom a lot more. So was I. It took us a long while to learn how to be clean. We had to learn that you couldn't just wash the parts you could see, but had to wash your ears and your hair once in a while, too, and clean your finger-nails with a knife or a bent paper clip or something. We helped each other. If I saw that Helen's ears were dirty or something, I'd tell her. She would make me comb my hair in the morning before we went to school. We weren't just being nice to each other either. We wanted to make sure that the other one didn't disgrace us. But I figured it was worth the trouble, because once we got clean, the other kids would finally like us.

It was harder to keep Mom and Dad from disgracing us. We didn't dare tell Mom to start washing our clothes more often. We just started doing them ourselves, washing our jeans and things out in the bathtub and hanging them on chairs and things to dry. It took us awhile to learn about that, too: that you couldn't just wash things out once every couple of weeks but had to do it all the time. We never knew what Mom thought about it. She must have known we were washing our own clothes, because they were hanging all over the place. But she never said anything, and I figured that she never felt guilty about it or anything—she just figured that kids ought to be responsible for washing out their own clothes. But I knew that the other kids in the third grade didn't wash their own clothes.

We couldn't get mad at Mom, because she had something wrong with her. I never knew what it was. I guess nobody ever knew what it was. She just seemed to be tired all the time. Dad was always taking her over to the county hospital for tests and checkups. They never could cure her. She had to sit around a lot in her bathrobe and watch TV. Sometimes Helen had to make supper, because Mom was too tired. So we didn't blame Mom for not washing our clothes—she couldn't help it.

So anyway, after a while we started being clean, but it didn't help us very much. The other kids still weren't too interested in doing anything with us. We didn't have any friends. For one thing, they said that the Whites stole. Once when I was in sixth grade I came into the cafeteria with my lunch bag. There was an empty seat near where a bunch of kids were sitting at a table eating. I went over and sat down. There was a watch lying on the table, and when I sat down, some kid said, "Don't touch that watch, White," and snatched it up.

"I wasn't going to touch your watch," I said. "What do I want to touch your watch for?"

"Everybody knows your family steals."

"What?" I said.

"Your sister steals stuff out of the drugstore. My sister said so."

"That's a lie," I said. I was beginning to lose my temper.

They all turned toward me, getting ready to gang up on me. "Oh, yeah? What about the chain saw your dad stole from the Otto brothers?" The Otto brothers owned the biggest gas station in town.

"Jim Otto was wrong," I shouted. "Dad bought that chain saw from somebody."

"Oh, yeah?" the kid said. "The cops told my dad it was Jim Otto's chain saw all right, but they couldn't prove it."

"That's a lie," I said. I jumped up and started to go for the kid, but Mr. Creasy came over and broke it up. "Take your lunch into the janitor's room, White," Mr. Creasy said.

"He started it," I said. I was sore and breathing hard.

"Don't give me that," Mr. Creasy said. "Go eat in the janitor's office."

But the truth was, I wondered. I sat there in the janitor's office with the mops and buckets all around, smelling the soap and the disinfectant and such, mixed in with the smell of my peanut butter sandwiches, and thinking about the time Jim Otto had come out to the house with the cops. That afternoon Dad had brought home an almost new chain saw. He said he'd bought it from a guy who'd got a bigger one and sold this one to Dad cheap. I was pretty excited about it, and I got Dad to promise he'd teach me how to use it. While we ate supper I kept looking over at it sitting on the kitchen floor. It was bright red, clean, and solid. It excited me. And we were just getting finished with supper when there was a knock on the back door. Dad went to answer it and found Jim Otto standing there with a cop.

Otto pointed at the chain saw. "There it is," he said. "That's it." He started to push past my dad to get the saw.

My dad grabbed Jim Otto by the arm. "Oh, no you don't," he said, as calm as could be. "You don't walk into a man's house without his permission. Out you go."

Jim Otto looked my dad in the face. He was pretty red and sore. "That's my saw, White. I got witnesses who saw you out back of my store this afternoon."

It amazed me how calm Dad was staying. "That doesn't alter the fact that you need a search warrant before you come into a man's house. Now get out before I have you arrested for trespassing."

"That's my saw, White," Jim Otto shouted.

"I'm going to count to three," my father said. "If you're not out then, I'm going to have this officer arrest you."

"White—"

The cop took Jim Otto's arm. "Better come on outside, Jim," the cop said.

"I don't just mean outside," my dad said. "I mean off my property."

"Come on, Jim," the cop said. And they left.

They came back two days later with a search warrant, but the chain saw wasn't there anymore. "Somebody swiped it off the back of my truck," Dad told Jim Otto. "It wasn't your saw anyway."

Jim Otto was pretty sore, and he cursed Dad out

until Dad told him to shut his mouth or he'd shut it for him, and the cop made Jim Otto leave. The truth was, though, that nobody had stolen the chain saw from the truck. Dad had taken it over to Watertown and sold it for fifty dollars. I was disappointed that it was gone, because it was so pretty, not like Dad's old beat-up chain saw. I said, "Dad, if it was your saw, why did you have to sell it?"

"They were going to make trouble about it. Jim Otto's been out to get me for a long time. I don't need that kind of aggravation."

"Why is Jim Otto out to get you?"

"He thinks I cheated him on a load of cordwood. Which I didn't do."

Sitting there in the janitor's room, smelling the disinfectant and the peanut butter, I wondered: Would Dad really steal anything? I just didn't see how he could—my dad wouldn't steal things. I remembered how calm he was when Jim Otto and the cop came. If he'd really stolen that chain saw, he wouldn't be calm, would he?

But it was true about Helen shoplifting out of the drugstore, because every time she swiped something she called me into her room and showed me what she'd got. It made her feel good to shoplift stuff. I couldn't understand it. A couple of times I'd been with her in the drugstore when she was swiping stuff, and it made me feel nervous. But Helen got a kick out of it.

So people thought we were dirty and stole and were just in general no good because of the junkers rusting by the driveway and the paint peeling off the house. I finally learned that nothing we did to get the other kids to like us would do any good. I was in the sixth grade when I learned that. The science teacher had a bird-watching club that met after school on Wednesdays. They'd go someplace in his station wagon to watch birds. I figured if I joined it, maybe I could make friends with some of the other kids. So I signed up, and I went a couple of times. I really liked it. I got a bird book out of the library and began studying the birds. Then, on the third Wednesday, while we were waiting around after school for the science teacher to get his station wagon, I started to go into the boys' room. I opened the door and I heard one of the kids say to another one, "Let's get the front seat. I don't want to sit next to Stinky White."

It made me go red, and mad and sick inside all at once. I ducked out of there and out the side door and hid in the areaway. Around the side of the building I could hear the science teacher say, "Where's White? Has anyone seen White?" I heard the horn honk, and after a minute the station wagon drove away. I never went back to the club. I just studied birds on my own.

After that I realized that the other kids would never like us, and I decided to forget about it. At school I didn't try to belong to any gang. Helen and I were by ourselves. Oh, there were a couple of girls who would let Helen eat lunch with them—girls that she sat next to in class and had got to know a little. And if the guys were getting up a softball game at lunchtime, they couldn't stop me from playing if I decided to. But we didn't have any real friends. Nobody ever said to us, "Hey, what are you doing after school?" We generally went home after school every day because we didn't have anything else to do. It was like we'd got a black spot on us, and couldn't rub it off, no matter what we tried.

I stood there in the backyard looking at the house with the paint peeling off, knowing that Helen was upstairs in her room feeling lousy with herself and wishing now that she hadn't let those guys come over, and suddenly I got sore. It wasn't fair; it wasn't right. What had we ever done to anybody? I was mad at Charlie Fritz, and mad at Dad for not having a regular job, and mad at everybody. I smacked my fist on my leg so hard, it hurt, and gritted my teeth and said out loud, "I'm going to do something. I'm not going to be trash anymore."

TWO

Timber Falls was a poor kind of a place. It was way upstate New York in the Adirondack Mountains, and there were always stories in the *Timber Falls Journal* saying how American prosperity had passed the region by, and giving figures on unemployment that showed that the towns around there were a lot worse off than towns in other parts of the state.

Timber Falls wasn't much of a place anyway. Main Street had a railroad track running down one side of it and a row of buildings along the other side, mostly old brick buildings. There was the drugstore, the hardware store, a bank, Old Man Greenberg's Sports Center, a couple of supermarkets, and down at the end of Main Street the town hall. That was about it. The train station across from the row of stores by the railroad track was closed because hardly any trains went through there anymore. You couldn't buy a ticket to anywhere there. About the only trains that came through were freight cars going up to the carpet factory.

The carpet factory was the big thing. A lot of people in Timber Falls worked there. Dad always said that if the factory ever closed, the town would just dry up and blow away. Mom was always trying to get Dad to go to work there so as to have a regular job, but Dad wouldn't. He would say that he wasn't ready to be anybody's slave yet.

The other thing was the mountains. They were everywhere you looked. You could stand in the middle of town and look all around, and everywhere you saw mountains. All year long they changed colors: brown in the spring, then going yellow as the trees budded and then light green as the buds came out, and dark green as summer came on; and in the fall going red and yellow and then brown once more when the leaves fell; and then white when the snow fell. They were always changing.

Rich people came up to hunt in the mountains in the fall. Leastwise, they seemed rich to me. Most of them had two or three expensive guns and fancy tents and cookstoves. Dad said, "I wish they'd stay where they belong, and keep away from here." But most people said they brought in money—buying shells at the hardware store, and steaks at the supermarket, and whiskey at the Liquor Mart.

It was beautiful up in the mountains. Sometimes, when Dad was in a cheerful mood, he'd take me up there. He'd fill a thermos bottle with coffee and pour in a slug of whiskey. We'd drive into town and get two big roast beef sandwiches and a Coke for me at

Red's Deli. Then we'd drive up into the mountains on the winding tar road, park the car on a dirt tote road, and hike on up to this place Dad knew about, where there was a rock cliff that jutted out of the side of a mountain. Up there you could see for miles and miles out over the Adirondacks. There was nothing out there but mountains and woods, and nothing in the woods but birds, deer, bear, and fish in the streams and lakes. We'd sit there and eat our roast beef sandwiches, and Dad would drink his coffee and whiskey, and we'd talk. "It's a satisfying view," Dad said one time. "No people."

"Why don't you like people, Dad?"

"Wait'll you know them better. I've been knowing people for forty years, and the less I have to do with them the better. Look at 'em all, robbing and cheating and stealing, so a man can hardly make a living. And then if you have anything left, they tax it away from you."

It didn't seem to me that it was everybody else's fault that Dad didn't have a regular job, but I didn't say that. "I thought you said you didn't have to pay any taxes," I said.

He gave me a look. "When did I say that?"

"A while ago," I said.

"Well, you just forget about that, Harry. Just forget I ever said it."

So I changed the subject and we talked about the hunters and deer, and Dad said maybe he'd get a couple of shotguns and we'd go after deer ourselves. But I knew he never would. Mom never knew how much he had. If she needed money for food, she would ask for it, and he would grumble and give it to her.

Actually I didn't go hiking with Dad in the mountains all that much. When you got down to it, I don't think it happened more than two or three times. Mostly Dad was quiet and kept to himself and didn't do much with the rest of us. He left in the morning without saying much. Mostly what he did was odd jobs. He'd truck stuff for people—pick up their trash when they had a big housecleaning, or move their furniture for them when they moved. Sometimes he did a little tree work, sometimes he'd do house painting, sometimes he'd do carpentry. He'd do anything so long as it wasn't regular and didn't last more than a week. Every time Mom got on him about going to work in the carpet factory, he would say that he couldn't stand being regimented like that. It was all right for the middle class with their fancy sofas and washing machines, but he had more spirit than that.

Mom was thirty-four and Dad was forty-two. Dad had been married once before, but we didn't know anything about that. Being as Mom and Dad had been married for seventeen years, you would have thought Mom would have known better than to get on Dad about a job, but she never gave up. She started in on him that night after Helen let those guys come over. She was opening some cans of Heinz beans. We were going to have franks and beans again. We ate a lot of stuff like that—franks and beans, canned hash and eggs, cold cuts, spaghetti and meat sauce out of a can—because, as Mom always said, it was cheap and nourishing. But Helen said it was because she would rather watch TV than cook. It was because of her being tired so much, I figured. Helen got her looks from Mom. She said Mom could be pretty if she took some trouble over herself.

Anyway, that night Dad came in through the kitchen door at supper time and said, "The clutch is going on the truck. The whole truck is going. They're going to make me buy at least two new tires to pass inspection this year. That's a hundred bucks even if I can find some used ones. I'll have to put four, five hundred dollars into it just to get through the rest of the year."

"That's good money after bad," Mom said. She was standing at the stove in her bathrobe and furry slippers, stirring the beans. It was an old gas stove, and the pilot lights didn't work anymore. You had to be careful about lighting it, because sometimes it would light down inside somewhere instead of on the burner.

Dad sat down at the kitchen table. It was an old pine table Mom had bought for ten dollars once and painted blue. It had been pretty when it was just painted, but it had got all scratched up since. "When's supper?" Dad said. "I'm hungry." He started to take off his boots.

"Soon," she said. "Frank, maybe you should give up the truck."

He looked at her. "Doris, how am I going to make a living without the truck?"

"You could take a job at the carpet factory."

"I figured that was coming," he said. "No way. I'm not about to make myself somebody's slave yet."

"It's good money, Frank."

"I don't care about the money. Besides, why should I add to the world's pollution?"

"I don't see why that's your worry, Frank."

"It ought to be everybody's worry," Dad said. He took off his socks and rubbed his foot. "These boots never did fit right."

I said, "I wondered where that stuff in the river was coming from. It's from the carpet factory."

"It sure is," Dad said. "Of course, they won't admit it."

"I thought it was against the law to pollute."

"It is," Dad said. "But people like them don't pay any attention to the laws. They're arrogant, those biggies with their Cadillacs and fancy houses. They run the factory anyway they want, regardless of the law. They do *anything* they want regardless of the law. They cheat the workingman, they cheat the public with lousy goods, they pollute, then they get some fancy accountants to figure out a way to get out of paying taxes on their money. No way I'm going to go out there and work for guys like that."

"Harry," Mom said, "where's Helen?"

"She's up in her room," I said.

"Tell her supper's ready," Mom said.

I went upstairs and into Helen's room. She was still lying on her bed. "You're supposed to knock before you come in," she said. She was in a pretty bad mood.

"Why do you let those guys come over if it always makes you feel bad?"

"It's none of your business," she said.

"Someday Dad's going to catch you and he'll kill those guys."

"I said it was none of your business," she said.

"Supper's ready," I said.

She went on lying on her bed. "Two more years," she said. "Two more years and I'll graduate and then I'm going to get out of here so fast, nobody'll believe it."

"Where would you go?"

"I don't know," she said. "Anyplace, so long as it isn't Timber Falls."

I didn't want her to go. I knew I would miss her. She was about the only person I had to talk to. "Don't you think you'd get homesick?"

"For this dump?"

"Well— But I mean for Mom and Dad." I really meant for me.

"Them?" She spit when she said it. "What have they ever done for us?"

"Well, still," I said. I was hoping she would say she would miss me.

But she didn't. "I hate them," she said.

That made me feel kind of funny. "You don't really hate them," I said.

"Yes, I do," she said. "Yes, I do."

"Still," I said. "Anyway, supper's ready."

After dinner Mom turned on one of her shows and sat there watching it with Helen. But it wasn't interesting to me, so I went out and sat on the back steps and watched it grow dark; I saw the sky go deep blue, and finally the stars came out. The peepers were going like mad, too, and the air had that damp spring smell to it.

I liked watching the stars come out. I would pick out a part of the sky that had no stars yet, a place where there was nothing but that deep blue. I would stare at it and stare at it, and all of a sudden there'd be a star there. It was like magic.

I did that a few times, until I got tired of it, and then I started to think about Helen going away. She had two more years of high school, and I had three. She talked a lot about what she was going to do after she graduated. Sometimes she said she wanted to go to school to become a dental technician. They made good money, she said, and she could have a nice apartment or condo or something, with wall-to-wall carpets and a big color TV and nice furniture, the way it was in some of the other kids' houses. Sometimes she said she was going to go to Hollywood and try to make it in the movies. That idea worried her, though, because she didn't think she was pretty enough. I would tell her she was pretty, but she had a hard time believing it. She would say, "No, I'm not pretty. My nose is wrong and my mouth is too big and my hair is always funny." When she was in that mood, she would decide to be a dental technician.

When I graduated, I was going to go into the air force. There was a reason for that: If you were in the air force, nobody could say you were trash. It wouldn't matter that I stunk in the third grade, or that the paint was peeling off our house and my dad didn't have a regular job. If you were in the air force, nobody could say you were trash. The thing was, you needed a high school degree to get into the air force.

I never told Mom and Dad about my plan. I knew what Dad would say about it. He would say that going in the air force was a sucker's game. I would just be cannon fodder for the biggies who ran the country.

I wondered: Did Helen really hate Dad and Mom? Or did she just say that because she was in a bad mood? I didn't hate them. Sometimes I got mad at them for things they did, but I didn't hate them. Mom was okay, really. She tried her best to do things right. It was only that she was tired so much. Dad was okay, too, sometimes. I just wished he wouldn't talk about the biggies all the time. I never knew whether to believe him when he talked about them cheating everybody and polluting the Timber River and such. I wished I knew if he was right.

He was right that there was pollution in the Timber River, though. I knew because times when I'd be lying by the river looking at the fish, just watching them flash around, changing direction all in an instant, I'd see on the top of the water flashes of red and green and yellow. It was some kind of chemicals, or oil or something.

But how did Dad know that it was coming from the carpet factory? Wouldn't the police or somebody have made them stop if they were really polluting the river? I knew it was against the law, because we'd studied it in social studies. It probably wouldn't be too hard to find out, I figured. The stuff would be coming out of a pipe or something. The carpet factory was right next to the river, so it would be easy to run a pipe from the factory to the riverbank. Of course, I didn't *know* that was the way they would do it, but it made sense. It wouldn't be hard to find out either. You could just go out there and walk along the riverbank until you saw the pipe or whatever it was. Something like that would be easy enough to spot.

Suddenly it came to me that I could go out there and look for the pipe myself. I could find out if Dad was right—that the carpet factory really was polluting the river. If they were, I could report it to the police, and they'd make the factory stop it. There'd be a big story in the *Timber Falls Journal* about me. I'd be a hero. The other kids at school would want to be friends with me, and nobody would say I was trash anymore.

I began to get really excited. The more I thought about it, the better an idea it seemed. All I had to do was find that pipe. What would be so hard about that? I was so excited, I couldn't sit there anymore but started walking around on the lawn.

Would I really have the guts to do something like that? Or would it be one of those things that you just *think* you're going to do and never get around to actually doing? It was exciting thinking about it, though, and I walked around going over it all in my mind: how I would go out to the river, walk up and down the bank until I found the pipe, and then go and get the police and the reporters and stuff. They'd take pictures of me and write a story about it in the papers. It was exciting thinking about it. But after awhile a little spring breeze came up, and it got chilly and I went in.

In the morning I had to finish my geometry homework while I was eating my breakfast, and I didn't have a chance to think about tracking down the river pollution. I had only got my geometry half done when Dad said, "Harry, I want you to bury the garbage this morning." The town garbage trucks didn't come out that far, so we took it out into the woods and buried it.

"The bus is coming soon," I said.

"You can skip school for once," he said.

"I can't, Dad," I said.

"It's a waste of time anyway. If it was me, I'd close the schools down and put all those lazy so-and-sos to work. What do you learn down there anyway? What's the use of that stuff?" He pointed to my geometry homework.

I knew that I would need to pass geometry if I wanted to go into the air force, but I didn't say that. "I have to pass it," I said.

"Frank," Mom said. "He has to go to school. It's the law."

"Forget about the law," Dad said. Then he got up, put on his jacket, and went out. In a moment we heard the truck start and go down the driveway.

Mom said, "You better come right home from school and do the garbage, Harry."

"Okay," I said. So, between everything, I didn't remember about the carpet factory and all that until I was on the school bus. There's a place where the Timber River runs alongside the road into town. The sun was bright and glinting on the water, and when I looked out at it, I remembered.

The whole idea of finding where the pollution was coming from was more scary in the daylight than it had been at night. It wasn't just something to have a daydream about, but real. The river was real and the carpet factory was real and the people who worked there were real. Maybe I ought to forget about the whole thing. Maybe it wouldn't make me into a hero anyway. Maybe I'd go on being trash.

Then I told myself I was just being chicken. I was just afraid of standing up to the grown-ups. What difference did it make that I was just a kid? What mattered was who was right, didn't it? But still, I felt nervous about it, and I wondered if I would really do anything about it.

I hadn't finished my geometry because of Dad interrupting me at breakfast, so I forgot about the pollution and worked on the geometry as best as I could with the school bus bouncing every which way. I didn't think about it again until lunch.

Our school was old because Timber Falls was poor. The cafeteria was in the basement. There were steam pipes overhead, and the fluorescent lights were on all the time because hardly any light came in from outside. The folding tables were all carved with initials, and there was always a sort of tomatoey smell down there.

Helen and I were supposed to bring our lunches instead of buying cafeteria food. Dad said there wasn't anything wrong with sandwiches, we needn't expect to be raised in the lap of luxury. Mostly I tried to remember to make my lunch the night before. There was usually enough stuff in the icebox to make good sandwiches out of—some leftover cold cuts or hot dogs, or baked beans. I liked cold baked bean sandwiches with a lot of mayonnaise. Cold hot dog sandwiches with catsup were good too. But if I forgot to make my lunch the night before, I would only have time enough to make peanut butter and jelly sandwiches. They were good, too, but you got tired of them after a while.

Helen never bothered to make a lunch. If she had some money, she bought a hot lunch in the cafeteria, and if she didn't, she'd beg something from somebody, mostly me.

When I came down to the cafeteria, I saw her sitting by herself at the end of a table, reading a romance. There were these two girls who would sit with Helen, but sometimes they were with other people, and Helen would be afraid to go over and sit with them in case somebody started making remarks. I never sat with anybody except Helen. If they didn't want me around, I wasn't going to make them. So I went and sat with Helen, and opened my lunch bag. "You still in a bad mood?" I said.

"I just felt like reading," she said.

"Don't you have any lunch?"

"No," she said. She went back to reading.

"You want half a sandwich?" I said.

"No," she said. "Can't you see I'm reading?"

"Don't you have any money?"

"Stop bothering me," she said. Then I saw her face get red. I looked around. Charlie Fritz was coming

slowly through the crowd carrying his tray and looking around for a place to sit.

"Charlie Fritz is coming," I said. She looked back
down at her book, but her face stayed red. "He's
coming right toward us," I said in a low voice.

Helen flicked up her eyes to look, and then looked
back at her book again. A little bit of sweat came out
on her upper lip, and she nervously licked it away.
She was still red. Charlie kept on coming closer. He
was looking around here and there, and I figured he
didn't see us. Helen flicked her eyes up to look at him
again, then flicked them back to her book. He was by
the next table now, standing there, still looking
around. Then he saw a place he wanted to sit, and
started to come right by us.

Helen looked up, and licked at the sweat on her
lips. Finally Charlie saw her. "Oh, hello, Helen," he
said.

"Do you want to sit here, Charlie?" she said.

"I guess not, Helen," he said.

She blinked. "Oh," she said. Her face went redder
than ever, and she looked back down to her book.
Charlie went on by and sat down with some guys a
couple of tables away from us. Helen kept her eyes
on her book, but she was hot and sweaty anyway. I
looked over to where Charlie was sitting with the
other guys. He was leaning forward, talking in a low
voice, and the other guys were leaning forward toward him. Every once in a while one of them would
take a quick look over at Helen. I wanted to go over

there and slug them. I wanted to start heaving dishes at them. I just hoped Helen wouldn't look up.

But she did. I guess she couldn't help herself. She looked up and she saw them, all leaning their heads together across the table, listening to Charlie; and two of them were staring right at her.

When they saw her looking, they snapped their heads away. Helen's face stopped being red and went pale white. She blinked and bit her lip. Then she closed her eyes, and the tears began rolling out of them.

"Helen," I whispered, "don't pay any attention to those guys."

She jumped up, threw her hands over her face so that nobody could see the tears, and ran out of the cafeteria as fast as she could go. I watched her run. Charlie Fritz and those guys stopped talking and watched her, and then everybody in the cafeteria was silent and watched her run through the tables with her hands over her face, bumping into chairs and things. Suddenly she was gone. For a moment the cafeteria was dead quiet, and I could hear the *tap-tap* of Helen's shoes as she ran up the cement cafeteria stairs. Then the cafeteria noise started up again. I picked up Helen's book and began pretending to read it, because I knew a lot of them would be staring at me. I didn't feel like finishing my lunch. I just wanted to get out of there, but I wasn't going to walk out in front of them all. So I sat until the bell rang and the place emptied out. I got up, darted up the cafeteria steps, and trotted away from school through the sunshine, feeling just terrible. There was one thing I didn't have any question about anymore: I was going to do something to show everybody in Timber Falls that we weren't trash.

THREE

I didn't really know where I was going. I just wanted to get away from school. I took the school road and then swung onto a side road where there wouldn't be much traffic. I was feeling sort of numb, and trying not to think about Helen. Instead, I thought about the pollution in the Timber River.

If they were dumping stuff in the river, it had to be coming out of a pipe somewhere along the riverbank. All I had to do was walk along the riverbank until I found it, then get a camera from somewhere and take some pictures of the pollution coming out. I wasn't exactly sure what I would do with the pictures. I figured there had to be some sort of state agency in Albany that was responsible for pollution. Or maybe the police. Or maybe I would just give the pictures to the *Timber Falls Journal* and let them run a big story about it. Then I could send the story to the agency in Albany or whatever it was.

In fact, that seemed like the best idea. They were

bound to take the whole thing more seriously if they saw a story about it in the paper than if some kid just sent in some pictures. That was the way to do it: Get the story in the paper first. Of course, I didn't have a camera, and neither did Mom and Dad. We'd never had one, as far as I could remember. In the ads on television families always have cameras and take pictures of their trips and vacations and kids' birthday parties and all that. We didn't go on any trips to take pictures of. Sometimes Dad went off for a few days or a week. He always said it was for a job out of state, but he never said where it was, or what it was, and we never knew for sure. But the rest of us never went on trips, so we couldn't have had pictures of them even if we'd had a camera.

We had birthdays, though. I mean, we didn't have real birthday parties with other kids coming over and balloons and hats and stuff. On our birthdays Mom would buy us a present—a toy or a doll or something when we were little, a sweater or a jacket when we were bigger. She would make something special for dinner that we liked—hamburgers and french fries or something—and she'd buy a cake and ice cream, and we'd blow out the candles and all that. But we never took any pictures of our birthdays, or Christmas or anything else. About the only pictures of myself I'd ever seen were one of Mom holding me when I was a baby, and another one that Helen and I took in a photograph machine once when we all went over to Watertown to see Mom when she was in a hospital for tests.

So getting hold of a camera was going to be a problem, but I figured I could solve it some way. I'd think about it for a while and see what came to me.

No matter how I tried to change the subject in my head, I couldn't help thinking about Helen. I didn't think she had gone home. If she came home early, Mom would want to know why, and Helen sure wouldn't want to tell her. I figured she would hang out someplace until three-thirty when we usually got home. I felt sorry for her. Going back to school the next day and facing everybody was going to be hard for her.

The truth was that it was Helen's own fault. I knew that. If she hadn't let those guys come around, none of it would have happened. But I guess she wanted so much to have some guys come to see her, she couldn't stop herself.

Still, I felt bad for her. What had happened to her wasn't right and it wasn't fair, and if Dad had only got a real job and a real house, maybe things would have been different. But there wasn't any use thinking about that. It wasn't Dad's way. He was his own man, he always said. He wasn't going to spend his life taking orders from the middle class. The whole thing confused me a lot. It wasn't fair for Helen; but why should Dad have to get a real job just for Helen?

I wondered what time it was. I couldn't go home either, not until three. But I had to go someplace where no cop was likely to come along and ask me why I wasn't in school. I would have to get away from town. And suddenly, just like that, I decided I would go out to the carpet factory just to have a look around.

I didn't know much about the place. I'd gone out there two or three times with Dad when he had something to deliver and needed help unloading. It was a big one-story cement block building with a corrugated iron roof. It had been there a long time—forty years maybe. Behind it there was a blacktop parking lot, which ran down to the Timber River. That was about all I knew about it.

I could get from the school road to the carpet factory without going through town. So I headed on out, going as quick as I could. In a little while I came to the road that ran along the Timber River out to the carpet factory. It was pretty out there. The river was boiling along with the spring rush, and the mountains stood all around me. Sometimes the road swung in close to the river so that it was not more than fifty feet from the bank; other times it swung away from it, so there was maybe a quarter of a mile of woods between the river and the road, and I couldn't see the river at all, or hear it boiling along either. It was only a couple of miles out to the factory, and after a while I began to get close.

Here the road was a good way from the river, with the woods in between. I kept on going, and pretty soon I came to an eight-foot-high steel mesh fence running along beside the road. I stopped and in a minute I realized that the fence turned the corner there and ran off down through the woods toward the river. I knelt down pretending to tie my shoe and took a look to see if anybody was around. A car was coming up the road. It slowed down when it came to me, but then it went by. I waited until it was out of sight, and then I slipped into the woods and worked my way along the steel mesh fence down to the river. I stopped on the riverbank and looked through the fence. It turned the corner again here and ran along the riverbank upstream in the direction of the carpet factory. It was pretty clear that the mesh fence must go all around the factory. I looked up at the top of the fence. There was barbed wire along the top. I could come back here with a pair of Dad's wire cutters and get through that easily enough, but I had a hunch that it would set off an alarm if you cut the barbed wire.

I turned back and looked at the river. Here, this close to the factory, the water had a kind of greenish tint to it, and the little spots of foam on the surface didn't look to me like ordinary whitecaps. I decided to take a look at the factory itself. I went back to the road and began walking along again. In a couple of minutes the woods ended, and there was the factory, about fifty yards back from the road, with a little lawn and some bushes out front, and behind it, as much as I could see from my angle, the parking lot and the loading docks. There were maybe a hundred cars in the parking lot.

The steel mesh fence went right along the whole thing and disappeared into more woods on the other side. It would go all the way around, I figured. There was a big steel mesh gate in the middle of the fence, where the factory road went in. The whole place was pretty well guarded, and I wondered why. I figured there was always the risk of thieves.

Anyway, it was going to be pretty impossible to get

in there and prowl around looking for the pollution pipe. How was I going to find it? Then it came to me that if I crossed the river, and went along on the opposite bank, I would see it. I didn't know how big a pipe you needed for something like that, but, I figured, from the amount of pollution that was in the water, it couldn't be some little piece of one-inch pipe. It would be a twelve-inch pipe or something. It wouldn't be hard to spot something that big sticking out of the riverbank.

I looked up at the sun, and judged that it must be getting on toward three, so I started for home, feeling a whole lot better. It felt good to be working on something interesting like this. It was sort of scary, too: but what was the danger? It wasn't going to be much of a problem going along the opposite riverbank trying to spot that pipe, I figured.

Mom was sitting at the kitchen table drinking a cup of coffee. She had a dress on, like she was going somewhere. "Where have you been, Harry? I've been so scared. My heart's been pounding so, I thought I'd have an attack."

I began to feel scared myself. "What's the matter? I've been at school."

"No, you haven't," she said. "They called from school. They said that you and Helen ran off after lunch. I've been so worried."

"Ran off?" I didn't know what to say.

"That's what they said. Where's Helen?"

"I don't know," I said. I wasn't worried about Mom so much as Dad. Mom wasn't much for punishing us. Dad always told her that she had to bear down on us harder. But Dad would hit you if he got mad enough. Suddenly I saw a way out. "I don't know where Helen went. I was looking for her."

"Harry, they said Helen was upset."

I didn't know what to say, but I had to tell her something. "She was crying in school," I said.

"Crying? What was she crying for?"

"I don't know," I said. "She was just crying."

"She didn't say where she was going?"

"She didn't say anything. I went looking for her, but I couldn't find her. I figured she came home."

"Where did you look?"

"Just around town," I said.

She took a sip of her coffee. "I'm so worried," she said.

"I have to bury the garbage before Dad gets home," I said.

I went outside, picked up the garbage can from behind the house, and toted it past the barn up into the woods. About a hundred feet in, there was a pit I'd dug for the garbage. We would dump the garbage in and cover it over with some dirt so that the animals wouldn't get into it. About every three months I would have to cover over the garbage pit with the dirt that was left, and dig a new one. The pit was pretty full. I was going to have to dig a new one pretty soon. I hate that: it was hard work and took a morning.

I dumped the garbage into the pit and shoveled dirt over it. I wondered where Helen was. I'd figured she'd come on home after three-thirty, but she wasn't home yet. I didn't know what that meant. I didn't think she'd go to visit those two girls who liked her, because she'd have to tell them what she was crying about. Where else would she go? If it had been me, I'd have gone off into the woods someplace to take my mind off it, but Helen wasn't much for going into the woods. Where could she be?

I wished Dad would come home with the truck so we could go out looking for her. Mom ought to be doing something. She didn't have a car, but she could be trying to find out where Dad was, to tell him. Or she could be phoning around to people to see if anyone had seen her. Or she could call the police. Do something, instead of just sitting there drinking coffee and worrying. That was the trouble with Mom: There didn't seem to be much to her.

I finished up the garbage and carried the can back to the house. Helen still wasn't home. I hosed the garbage can out so it wouldn't stink. Then I went up to my room so as to be where Mom couldn't start asking me questions. All my schoolbooks were still in my locker at school where I'd put them at lunchtime, but I was supposed to be writing a report on the ecology of the Adirondacks, which I knew a lot about anyway. So I started on it.

But I couldn't concentrate. The longer the day went on, the more I worried about Helen. Why wasn't she coming home? It began to grow dark, and still she didn't come. She always came home by supper time. There wasn't much else for her to do. I told myself that she was just messing around somewhere, and tried to concentrate on my report. Then I heard Dad's truck drive in and stop. The door slammed.

Maybe Helen had got a ride home with Dad. I jumped up and ran to the window. It was just Dad. He took his toolbox out of the back of the truck and carried it up to the barn. Then he came back down to the house and went in. I jumped up and went downstairs. Mom was still sitting at the beat-up blue kitchen table drinking coffee. Dad was standing in the middle of the kitchen. He said, "What do you mean she's run off?"

"They called from the school. She was crying and ran out of school. Harry went looking for her, but he couldn't find her."

"Crying?" Dad said. "What was she crying about?"

"I don't know," Mom said. She looked like she was about to cry herself.

Dad looked at me. "What's this all about, Harry?" he said.

"I don't know," I said. "I think she was pretty upset about something."

Mom started crying. "I don't know what we're going to do, Frank."

Dad sat there for a minute, frowning and thinking. Then he said, "It probably wasn't anything. Nerves or something. Let's eat."

Mom tried to stop crying, and wiped her eyes with a tissue.

"No, Frank, something's wrong. It isn't like her. I just know something's wrong."

"You're making a big thing out of nothing. She probably had some trouble with her boyfriend. It'll all blow over. Let's eat." He sat down at the table.

Mom stood up and faced him. "Frank—"

"Stop worrying. She's probably made it up with the guy already, and she's fooling around with him and forgot the time. She's sixteen. She isn't a baby. So what if she's ten minutes late."

"Please, Frank, please."

He sighed. "All right," he said. "All right. Come on, Harry, let's go find her."

We weren't going to find her. By now I knew that she'd run away. Where, I didn't know. But I knew that she wasn't around Timber Falls anymore. I didn't say anything; I just got my jacket, and we went out into the truck. Dad started the engine. "Where does she usually hang out?"

"Mostly everybody goes to Teddy's Pizza Parlor," I said. Helen went there sometimes, I knew, but she usually didn't have enough money, not unless she could borrow some. We drove into town and stopped at Teddy's, which was between the hardware store and the liquor store. "See if she's in there," Dad said.

I didn't want to because everybody in there would know who I was looking for. But I couldn't argue with Dad, so I got out of the truck and went into Teddy's. Charlie Fritz was there, sitting at a booth fooling around with a couple of guys. He looked at me, but he didn't say anything. I turned around, went out, and got back into the truck. "She isn't there," I said.

"Where else is she likely to be?" he said. "Who's her boyfriend? Maybe she's over at his house."

"She doesn't have— She isn't going with anyone right now," I said.

"She doesn't have a boyfriend?" he said. "A girl

that pretty doesn't have a boyfriend? What about her girlfriends?"

"I don't know, Dad," I said. "She doesn't have too many friends."

"That can't be right, Harry," he said. "She must have friends. She's pretty and smart, she ought to have lots of friends."

"She doesn't have too many friends," I said.

"I don't understand that," he said. "I just don't understand it."

He didn't know anything about Helen. He didn't know anything about who she was, or what she did, or what her life was like. What could I say to him? How could I explain to him that the whole time Helen was in elementary school she stank? How could I explain to him that everybody we knew thought we were trash?

We drove around town for a while, looking into the stores that were still open, and then we drove home. Dad didn't say very much but just looked straight ahead all the way home.

FOUR

After Helen had been missing for two days, Dad went down to the cops and told them about it. They put in a missing person report and told him not to worry, teenagers were always running off and usually came back by themselves. When Dad came home, he told Mom, "It's just a phase or something. She'll come back. Give her a few days of missing her meals and she'll come back." Then after that he seemed to forget all about her.

But Mom didn't. She moped around the house worse than ever. She could hardly get herself to cook —all she'd do was open some cans of stew or something and heat it up on the stove. I could tell that Dad didn't like it, but he didn't say anything. She even stopped watching TV. Mostly she sat at the kitchen table in her bathrobe drinking coffee. At night she just picked at her food.

"I can't stand watching you pick at your food like

that," Dad said. "Stop worrying, she'll come home soon."

To tell the truth, seeing Mom so low all the time got on my nerves too. Once I went into Helen's room looking for a pencil, and I caught Mom sitting on Helen's bed, holding Helen's sweater in her hands and smelling it. "My poor baby," she said when I came in. "I'm so worried about her."

I was worried about her too. I knew that she didn't have any money, because she hadn't had enough for lunch the day she ran away. She hadn't taken any clothes either. They were all still in her room where she'd left them. How was she going to live with no money and no clothes?

I wondered where she'd gone. Farther downstate, I figured—Rochester, or Albany, or maybe even New York City. I'd been down to Rochester on a school trip to see a science exhibit that one of the photograph companies there put on, but I'd never been to New York. Helen had been to New York once on a school trip; they saw some Shakespeare play and spent the night in a big hotel. When she came back, she was all excited about New York—how big it was and how many people there were there, and the wonderful things that the stores were packed full of. She couldn't get over the stuff in the shop windows— books and records and cameras and clothes and hi-fis and silverware, anything you could think of. So she might have gone to New York. You could hitch there in a couple of days. But what would she eat while she was hitching?

I really missed her. We used to fight a lot, but when

you got down to it, she was the only person I had to talk to. We talked about Mom and Dad a lot—about Mom being sick all the time, and Dad not having a regular job, and us being poorer than everybody else. We talked about why we never saw our relatives. Dad's brother lived out in California, and he had children that were our cousins. We knew what they looked like, because we'd usually get a Christmas card from them with a photograph on it. There were two girls and a boy, and they were eight, eleven, and thirteen. We wondered what they were like, and what their life was like in California. Mom said that Dad's brother did real well—he was a foreman in a printing plant out there and made a lot of money. Dad said that was okay if you didn't mind being regimented, but it wasn't for him.

Mom's parents lived in Binghamton. They were our grandparents, but we never saw them, even though it wasn't more than a couple hundred miles down there. We never got a Christmas card from them, and Mom didn't talk about them very much, and not at all when Dad was around, so we didn't know much about them. But once I heard Mom talking to them on the telephone—I don't know how I knew it was them, but I knew. Afterward Mom cried and cried. Mom would talk to Helen about them more than she did to me. Helen said that our grandfather was sixty years old and was a carpenter. The whole thing was, they didn't like Dad, Helen said.

So we didn't know much about Mom's parents, but we didn't know anything at all about our other grandparents, Dad's folks. He hardly ever said anything about them at all. Once when we drove out into the mountains and he was in a good mood, I asked him where they lived.

"Out in Oklahoma," he said. "They were mean and I never got along with them. My old man put me to work in the fields when I was fourteen, and I ran away after that as soon as I could." But that's all he would ever say about them.

Helen and I talked about things like that a lot, but one subject we didn't talk about was being trash. We just didn't say anything about it to each other. I wouldn't have minded talking about it, but Helen didn't want to. Every time I started to get into it, she would say that I was exaggerating or something. She would admit that we were poorer than most people in Timber Falls, and that our house was junky, but she wouldn't admit that everybody in town thought we were trash. The reason why she didn't have any boyfriends, she said, was that she wasn't pretty enough, or didn't have the right personality, or didn't have nice clothes. Each time it was something different. After a while I stopped trying to talk to her about it.

Even so, we talked about most things, and we did a lot of things together. When Helen was in the third grade, and I couldn't read yet, she would read me stories in bed when we were supposed to be asleep. She'd come into my room with a library book and get into bed with me, and read to me in a low voice so Mom and Dad wouldn't know we were awake. I really liked that, having somebody to snuggle up to; and I'd listen and get sleepy, and finally I'd doze off

and Helen would say, "You fell asleep again, Harry."
And I would say, "No, I didn't, I just closed my eyes."
Then she would make me tell what had happened in
the story, and of course I couldn't, and she would say
that she wasn't going to read to me anymore. But she
always did.

When we got older, we used to play cards in the
afternoon when there wasn't anything else to do. We
played go fish and old maid mostly. For a while we
had a Monopoly set. I don't know where it came
from. It wasn't whole: we had to use buttons for the
pieces, and there wasn't the right amount of money,
but we played it anyway. Sometimes the game would
go on for days, and of course, we always ended up
fighting. I don't know what happened to the Monopoly set. After a while it was gone.

Sometimes on the weekends, if Dad wasn't around
giving us jobs, we went bike riding. Helen got her
bike first, when she was around eight. Dad said bikes
were a middle-class luxury he couldn't afford, but
Helen begged and pleaded with Mom, and finally
Mom got Dad to get Helen a bike. It was a beat-up
old Schwinn that he'd got used somewhere. Helen
found some paint out in the barn and painted it. She
painted the fenders blue and the frame red and the
seat yellow. I sat in the barn watching her. By the
time she was finished she had blue and red and yellow all over her—her hands, her face, her ears, her
hair. She thought the bicycle was beautiful, and so
did I at the time. I was only about six then, and it
seemed to me just the smartest idea to paint the bike
different colors. A couple of years after that Helen

got a better bike. It was a bike somebody's kids had got too big for, and they gave it to Helen. I guess they felt sorry for her. So Helen gave me her bike, and now it was my turn to paint it, and I made it all green, which was the kind of paint there was most of in the barn.

After that we took bike trips. I was maybe nine or ten, and she was twelve. We would make peanut butter and jelly sandwiches. If we had any money, we would buy Cokes and Devil Dogs or boxes of cookies. Then we would ride out to this place we knew of, where there was a stream coming down from the mountain. The road crossed over the stream on a little bridge, and down from the bridge in the woods a little way was a grassy place by the side of the stream. You couldn't see it from the road. We would go in there and be secret and tell each other what we were going to do when we were grown-up; and we would eat our lunch, and swim if it was really hot, for that mountain stream was pretty cold even in the middle of summer.

Then after a couple of years Helen began going to high school and got interested in guys, and we didn't do stuff together so much. But I remembered all the things we did. It made me sad to think of them, and I wished Helen would come back.

Having Helen run off like that just made the talk about us worse. The kids at school were curious, and they kept coming around and asking me where she had gone and what she was doing. Even the seniors and juniors kept asking me, guys that I hardly knew and that had never paid any attention to me before.

They'd come up to me and say, "Hey, White, I heard your sister ran off to California." Or they'd say, "Hey, White, I heard somebody saw your sister down in New York hanging around Times Square." Or they'd say, "Hey, White, I heard your sister got busted for drugs." They were hoping to find out something really bad about her. It didn't matter what it was, just as long as it was something bad.

I would answer, "It's none of your business." If it was some guy older than me, he'd tell me to watch my mouth, but he'd go away because he knew he shouldn't be asking private stuff like that. If it had been somebody else's sister, everyone would have been shocked and afraid to bring it up in public. But with us it didn't matter: it was just what you would expect.

So I stayed away from people as much as I could. But the whole thing made me more determined than ever to show everybody in Timber Falls that we were as good as they were.

I planned that I would go over to the other side of the river and look for the pollution pipe on the next Saturday. Dad would have work for me. He always did on Saturday. But he usually went off somewhere himself, so I'd be able to get away.

That was the way it worked out. He told me to get started on another garbage pit, which would be four feet deep in the middle, and ten feet across. So I went out right after breakfast with a shovel and a pick and began digging. It was going to be a pretty day—a warm spring day with a fresh, new smell in the air, and with birds swooping across the fields and through the woods, gathering twigs and grass for their nests. It would be a nice day to go exploring along the river. I dug away for a while, working up a pretty good sweat. Then I heard the truck start, and I tossed down the shovel and went back to the house, just in time to see the truck pull out of the driveway. I went into the house and made myself some lunch, for I figured I'd be gone until the afternoon. There was some sliced American cheese in the icebox, and a dish of cold string beans, which were pretty good in a sandwich if you put a lot of mayonnaise on them. Mom was watching TV, but she came out to the kitchen to see what I was doing.

"Where are you going?" she said.

"Out to look for birds," I said.

"Be sure to work on the garbage pit," she said, "or you'll get in trouble with Dad."

"I will," I said. "When I come back."

She looked at me, mighty sad. "You're a good boy, Harry. I hope you'll always be a good boy." I knew she was thinking about Helen.

"I'm not so good, Mom," I said. I put the sandwiches into a paper bag.

"My poor baby," she said. She was still thinking of Helen. "I can't understand what made her do it."

"I don't know, Mom," I said.

"Did she ever say we were treating her badly?"

"I don't think so," I said. "She never said anything like that." How was I supposed to tell the truth?

"It makes me feel so bad to think of her out there someplace all alone."

"I've got to go," I said.

"Be a good boy, Harry," she said.

I didn't usually bother to hitchhike into town, because people who knew who I was wouldn't pick me up in case I had cooties. But this time I tried it so as not to waste time, and a stranger came along and took me into the town.

The Timber River ran alongside the town about a quarter mile from the main street. Back in the old days, when there was a lot of logging in the Adirondacks, the river had been used for floating logs out to the sawmills. Timber Falls had grown up around the sawmills as a lumbering town. Actually there weren't any real falls there—just some rapids where the river ran down a steep slope below town. A road ran up each side of the river—a pretty good concrete road going out to the carpet factory on our side, and a beat-up old blacktop road running along the other side, where there were some dairy farms. To get to the old blacktop road, you went over the railroad tracks and then crossed the river on an old steel bridge painted silver.

So I did that; and when I got to the middle of the steel bridge, I stopped. I stood there, looking down at the river through the steel supports, feeling the sun on my back. There was stuff in the river all right— streaks of green, and patches of oil filled with wavering rainbow colors. The colors were pretty, but not if you knew what was causing them. If you knew, they were ugly.

I walked across the bridge and came to the blacktop that ran along this side of the river. The blacktop was all busted up because the farmers who lived farther out ran their tractors and harvesting machines along it. They weren't supposed to, but they did, and they broke up the blacktop pretty quickly.

I began to walk out along the blacktop. Along the riverside there were some trees, and along the other side, open fields, some of them filled with last year's corn stubble, some of them black dirt where the farmer had already plowed for this year's corn. After a bit the road veered away from the river, so that there was maybe a hundred yards of woods between the road and the river. You couldn't see the river at that distance, and you couldn't hear it either.

I went on for a while until I figured I was getting to a point opposite the carpet factory on the far bank. I took a look around, and when I didn't see anybody, or any cars coming, I slipped into the woods, moving as quick as I could to get to where I wouldn't be seen from the road. When I was far enough in, I slowed down and walked to the river. About ten feet from the riverbank I crouched down and looked out across the river. About fifty yards upstream on the other side I could see the steel mesh fence where it came down through the woods, turned, and then went along the riverbank.

I backed off into the woods a little bit, so anybody who happened to be on the opposite bank wouldn't see me, and began moving slowly along upstream. Every couple of minutes I'd stop and push back toward the riverbank to see what I could spot. I didn't see anything that looked like a pipe.

After a bit the woods on the opposite bank ended,

and there was the factory, sitting in the middle of the blacktop parking lot. Being as it was Saturday, there weren't many cars there—just a dozen or so. Some trucks were parked at the loading platforms. I didn't see any people.

I figured if there was a pipe, it would come out around there. I worked my way a little upstream until I was directly opposite the middle of the factory. Then I stopped and began looking along the opposite bank. It was hard to make out anything. The river was a couple of hundred feet across, and a lot of brush and weeds grew on the opposite bank.

I looked up at the factory to see if there was any sign of a pipe coming out of it. From where I was standing I could look into the factory and see the shapes of some machines. Still no people.

Then I noticed a security guard walking across the blacktop parking lot toward the river. I stood watching. He came all the way down to the steel mesh fence that ran along the river at the edge of the parking lot, and stood there, looking across the river.

Suddenly I realized that he was looking at me. I'd gotten too close to the riverbank. I froze. I was about five feet back into the woods, partly in the shadows and partly in the sunlight. There was no way I could tell whether he could actually make me out, or had seen movement and was just suspicious. I didn't move, and after a minute he turned and trotted off across the parking lot and disappeared around behind the factory.

Now what? Had he seen me? Was he going to call the police? Would he get into a car and come after me? That was a pretty scary idea. My view of the factory gate was blocked, and I wouldn't be able to see a security car driving out.

Still, I wanted to find that pipe. I took another good look along the riverbank opposite to where I was standing. Then I moved back into the woods a little, and continued on upstream the way I'd been going. Every fifty feet or so I dropped to my knees and crawled out to the riverbank as close as I dared, and scanned the bank opposite. I went on doing this until I was a half mile above the factory, and then I gave it up. If there was a pipe coming out of the riverbank, I missed it.

But I knew that the pipe had to be there, because when I looked down into the Timber River at the place where I was, which was a good bit upstream from the factory, the water was clear. There wasn't any green tinge to it, or any rainbowy patches of oil, the way there was farther down. They had to be dumping stuff into the river somewhere, and I couldn't see how they could do it except from a pipe. Probably they'd camouflaged it. What I needed was binoculars. I wondered if Dad knew anybody who had a pair of binoculars I could borrow. Anyway, the best thing was to give up for the day and see if I could get hold of some binoculars somehow. For one thing, I had to go home and finish the garbage pit.

I was worried about going home, though. I was afraid that the security guard might be out there on the beat-up blacktop road waiting for me to come out. Or maybe he'd called the cops, and they would come patrolling as I was walking along. I decided I'd better wait a little, so I pulled back into the woods out of sight of the river, sat down with my back against a big maple, and ate my sandwiches. They tasted pretty good after all that running around in the woods. Then I went carefully through the woods until I came to the road. I had a look around. There was nobody there, and so I started for home.

It was around three o'clock when I got back. Dad was already home. He was up in the barn working on something. I went on up and saw it was a sickle bar, for mowing fields. He'd got the parts carefully laid out on the old plank floor and was washing them off with kerosene from a coffee can.

The barn was pretty beat-up. The paint had been gone off it for years. The sides were gray, and the wood was so soft, you could scratch it with your fingernail. There were cracks where the boards had shrunk and warped, and a couple of the windowpanes were broken. Dad said he wasn't going to pay good money to fix up somebody else's barn.

Inside, along one wall, there was a long workbench with Dad's tools scattered on it. Most of the rest of the space in the barn was filled with Dad's junk. There was an old V-8 engine Dad had got somewhere, a couple of power mowers, some worn truck tires—oh, just a mess of stuff. And more was hanging from the beams above—coils of rope, pieces of chain, old fan belts, loops of wire. Dad liked junk.

Upstairs was the loft. There was some old furniture there that belonged to the people we rented it from: an old sofa, a couple of bureaus, some busted chairs—

things like that. The loft was where Helen would go with Charlie Fritz and those guys.

"Where'd you get the sickle bar, Dad?" I said.

"I bought it from some guy for fifty bucks. He couldn't get it to work." He didn't look up but went on cleaning the sickle bar parts.

"What are you going to do with it?"

"There's work around cutting fields," he said. "You can get twenty-five bucks an hour for that kind of work." Then he looked up at me. "Where've you been? I thought I told you to dig a garbage pit."

"I started it," I said. "I'm going to finish it up now. Listen, Dad, you don't have any binoculars, do you?"

He looked back at the sickle bar and began unbolting the engine from the carriage. "What do you need binoculars for?"

"For birds," I said.

He grunted. "If you need binoculars, Old Man Greenberg's got plenty of them in the Sports Center."

"I haven't got enough money to buy any. I keep trying to save, but I always have to spend it."

He didn't look up but went on twisting the nut with the end wrench. "I didn't say anything about buying them," he said.

For a moment I didn't get what he meant. Then I got it. I felt weird, like I'd suddenly been shifted into another place. "What?" I said. I couldn't think of anything else to say.

He went on swinging the end wrench round and round. "You heard me," he said.

"I couldn't do that," I said. I still felt weird.

"What do you think, you're better than everybody else?"

I began to grow hot, and to blush. "I just couldn't," I said.

He took the end wrench off the nut and unscrewed it with his fingers. But this time he looked at me. "Now you listen to me, Harry. Do you think those guys don't steal, those biggies with their Cadillacs and fancy houses? How do you think Old Man Greenberg got that Mercedes of his? How do you think that Herbst over at the carpet factory got that big house?"

I hated the idea that my father stole. I just wanted to get away from him. "I don't know," I said.

"They lie, cheat, and steal. That's how."

"But I don't see—"

"You don't see." He wasn't working on the sickle bar anymore. He was just kneeling there, looking up at me. "Well, I'll tell you how. They make deals with each other to underpay their workers, to fix prices and overcharge for the garbage they make, and when they pile up the dough, they get some smart accountant to get them out of paying taxes. Oh, you better believe it, Harry, these biggies are the real crooks. If the stuff they do ever came out, they'd all go to jail just like that. But it won't come out because they're in with the government, and the cops don't dare lay a finger on them. But let some poor working-man take a can of paint off a truck so he can support his family, they bang him in jail and throw away the key. That's what cops are for—to keep the working people in line. Did you know that, Harry? Did you know they invented the police to keep the poor from taking back what the rich stole from them?"

I felt like I was being smothered. I wanted to get away from him. "I didn't know that," I said.

"You think about it, Harry," he said. He started to work on the next nut. "Think about it."

I didn't say anything for a minute. Then I said, "Well, I better go dig the garbage pit."

I went out into the woods and began to dig, and while I dug, I thought about it. So Dad *had* stolen the chain saw from Jim Otto. I began to remember other things. Once Dad came in with a brand-new set of socket wrenches that was worth fifty or a hundred bucks. Once he came home with a little black-and-white TV because Mom had been complaining she couldn't see her shows on our old one. Once he came home with a pair of brand-new snow tires for the truck, still in their yellow paper wrappings. I remembered asking him why he hadn't had the tire store guy put them on the wheels, the way they usually do. He told me that the guy had been too busy. But now I knew.

It made me feel sick. Maybe we were trash after all. Maybe everybody in Timber Falls was right: The Whites were just plain no-good. Oh, we were clean now, and didn't stink. But what difference did that make if we stole? The thing that made me sickest about it was that everybody *knew* we stole. They hadn't caught Dad yet, but they knew. Jim Otto knew that Dad had stolen his chain saw, because he'd seen it sitting on our kitchen floor. Jim Otto had told it all over town, so everybody knew. And I was sure that there were other things. I was sure that when stuff was missing, people remembered that Dad had been around. So they knew, and it wouldn't do me any good to deny it, because it was true. We stole.

What about all that stuff Dad always talked about the biggies stealing from the working people? Was Dad right? Was it true? It sounded just like an excuse to me, but I didn't know.

Then I had another thought: Would I grow up to be like Dad? Would I become a crook too? Thinking that made me feel even worse. Look what happened to Helen: She had started to do wrong herself. Could it happen to me too? Would I start having temptations to steal that I couldn't control, the way Helen couldn't control herself when those guys came around? Maybe I would. The idea made me feel empty inside, and I decided to keep a close watch on myself, just to make sure I didn't take anything at all that didn't belong to me, even something as small as a paper clip.

FIVE

Two days later Dad came in at supper time and handed me a brand-new pair of binoculars. "Here," he said.

I took them and stared at him.

"Don't worry," he said. "I paid for them."

I knew I had to say thanks, but it was an awful struggle. "Gee, Dad, they're great."

"Don't lose them," he said. "They cost forty bucks."

"Gee, Dad," I said. "I won't lose them."

I took the binoculars up to my room, laid them on the bed, and sat next to them, staring at them. They were beauties all right. Seven by thirty-five, just right for bird-watching. For birds you don't want them too powerful because powerful glasses have a small field and you can't cover enough area. It thrilled me to look at them, so new, and sleek. I loved just looking at them. After a minute I picked them up. I loved holding them too. They felt heavy and firm.

I set them back down on the bed, and stared at them some more. For I hated them too. They scared me. Dad had stolen them, there wasn't any question about that. If he'd bought them, they would have come in a box with instructions and all that, not just plain like they were.

I took them outside to try them out while there was still some light. I slung them around my neck, climbed over the stone wall, went into the old pasture with the sumac and little cedars growing in it, and began looking at things. The binoculars were terrific all right. A couple of robins were building a nest, and I could bring them in so close it seemed like I could touch them. They were great binoculars, just what I needed for finding the pollution pipe.

But why should I bother with that anymore? I let the binoculars hang down from the strap. If everybody in Timber Falls knew we stole, would it make any difference what I did to stop being trash? And suppose I went out there to the factory and the cops came along and caught me with the binoculars?

I wondered who he'd stolen them from. Probably Old Man Greenberg. Although, when I thought about it, it wouldn't be easy to steal anything from the Sports Center. It was a pretty small store. Old Man Greenberg sold guns and tennis rackets and badminton sets and shotgun shells. From behind his counter he could see pretty much everywhere in the store. It wouldn't be easy to steal from there.

Maybe he had stolen them from some store over in Watertown. Or maybe he'd just happened to see them lying on the seat of somebody's car, and reached in and grabbed them. In Timber Falls people didn't usually lock their cars when they went into a store. It wouldn't be hard to steal from a car.

The more I thought about it, the more it seemed that he must have known where they were, and just gone and took them. He might have seen them in somebody's house when he was delivering cordwood or hauling away somebody's junk. Maybe he'd seen them hanging on a nail behind a bar somewhere. I just didn't know.

The problem was that I couldn't return them even if I decided to, because I didn't know who to return them to. And I couldn't walk around with them hanging around my neck, because at any moment I might run into the guy he'd stolen them from. And if I just hid them away and never used them, Dad would ask me why I wasn't using them, and I wouldn't have any good answer to that.

Anyway, I was afraid that Old Man Greenberg would suddenly turn up with a cop, the way Jim Otto had, so that night I hid the binoculars in the cardboard box where I kept my clothes. But no cops came that night, or the next night, and in a few days I stopped worrying about it. I hammered a nail into the window frame and hung the binoculars on it where I could see them when I was in bed. Whenever I got a chance, I practiced with them, focusing on birds, squirrels, and chipmunks out the window. And on the next Saturday I took them back out to the woods by the carpet factory.

I kept them buttoned under my jacket all the way. Even so, going through town, I was pretty scared that somebody might spot the strap around my neck, and the bulge under my jacket, and guess what it was. But nobody did, and I got out there okay. It was a cloudy, raw day, the kind where it looks like it might rain. I was glad of the weather, though, because it darkened the woods, and made it harder for anybody to see into them. I slid cautiously in among the trees, and then started along through them. In a few minutes I began to make out through the branches and tree limbs the shape of the factory across the river and the empty parking lot around it. I dropped flat and crawled forward over the dead leaves on the ground. When I was three feet from the riverbank, I stopped. I didn't dare go any farther, because I would be pretty easy to spot from the factory if anybody was looking.

I propped myself up on my elbows and raised up the binoculars. When I got them adjusted, I began to scan the whole factory, going from one side of the parking lot all the way across to the other—the blacktop, the cars, the cement block factory building, more blacktop. And I'd got just about that far when I saw the security guard. He was sitting on top of one of the loading platforms, smoking a cigarette. I could make him out pretty well through the binoculars. He was maybe in his fifties or something, and getting bald. A flashlight and nightstick hung from one side of his belt, and a pistol from the other. I wondered if he was allowed to shoot people who were trespassing. Anyway, he was a good long way from me, and I didn't think he would be able to see me in the woods, dark as they were, unless I started moving around in clear view. Just then he flung down his cigarette, jumped off the loading platform, and went off quickly around the building, out of sight.

I scanned the rest of the plant, moving the binoculars around until I'd covered every inch of the factory. I didn't see anything suspicious—no pipe running out of the side of the factory, no big valves and dials. That didn't surprise me very much. If they were dumping stuff in the river on the sly, they were sure to bury the pipe, or hide it some other way.

Now I began to work the binoculars slowly along the riverbank opposite, starting as far upriver as the first bend. It was pretty hard to make anything out, even with the binoculars, for there was brush growing out of the bank, rocks sticking out here and there, tree branches hanging down, and dead sticks that had fallen out of the trees. I went slowly, covering every inch of the bank as carefully as I could.

I didn't find anything—nothing that looked like a pipe jutting out of the riverbank. I was disappointed: I was sure that a pipe was there, somewhere. How else would that stuff get into the river?

So I started moving the binoculars along the bank again, going in the other direction this time, and suddenly, when I was searching pretty far upriver, I saw something. I held steady and readjusted the focus to make it as sharp as could be. There was something there all right, something that looked like a black shadow running down the riverbank. What interested me was that it had a straight edge. You don't see anything straight in the woods: everything is crooked, or curved, or wiggly.

I had to get a better look at it, so I crawled back into the woods, and then ran a little ways in a crouch upstream toward where I'd seen the straight-edged shadowy thing. When I was getting close, I dropped flat again and crawled out toward the riverbank, stopping a little way back in the shadow of the woods.

But when I raised the binoculars, I realized that I didn't have a very good angle on the shadowy thing. I crawled forward a little farther, then rose up to my knees, and focused the binoculars on the opposite bank. And just when I did that, I realized that the security guard was standing across the river by the steel mesh fence that ran along the riverbank. He'd spotted me all right. Worse than that, he could easily see that I was using binoculars.

"Hey you," he shouted across the water. "What're you doing there?" He put his hand on the butt of his pistol, but he didn't draw it.

I slid back into the woods, mighty scared. "Hey," he shouted again. "Come out of there. I want to know what you're doing."

I was out of his sight now, and I stopped to think. If I was going to get a good look at that shadowy thing, I'd have to go farther upstream. What if the security guard jumped into his car and came after me? What if he called the cops? I didn't want to be caught with these binoculars around my neck, that was for sure.

I stood there feeling worried and nervous. I couldn't decide what to do. It would take the security guard a good ten minutes to drive from the carpet factory into town, cross the steel bridge, and then come on up the beat-up blacktop road to where I was. If he phoned the police, they might get to me quicker, but not much quicker, unless they happened to be on patrol out there. Either way I had a little time, if I moved quickly.

So I told myself not to be chicken and began to jog through the trees upstream to get a better angle. I was pretty nervous, though, and every couple of minutes I'd stop to listen for the sound of cars, or somebody coming through the brush. But I didn't hear anything, and in a few minutes I figured I was far enough along to get a look at that straight-edged shadow.

I dropped into a crouch and slipped along toward the river until I could just begin to see it again through the trees. Then I fell flat and squirmed ahead on my belly, keeping a good eye out for anybody moving around across the river. When I got within four or five feet of the bank, I could see the opposite side well enough, and I slowly raised myself up and had a look back downstream to the place where I'd seen the security guard before. He was gone, and I knew that he was either calling the police or coming after me himself.

Now I raised up the binoculars and adjusted the focus. And right away I saw it—a black iron pipe about twelve inches in diameter sticking out of the riverbank at an angle that slanted down. There was brush all around it, which explained why I'd had such a hard time spotting it, and I figured they'd planted the brush there themselves for camouflage. But below the pipe there was a deep furrow in the bank where nothing grew. They'd been pouring some kind of chemicals out of that pipe, that was clear enough.

For a few minutes I knelt there looking at the pipe through the binoculars, hoping I'd see something come out. I was feeling pretty nervous, and I kept my ears open for sounds of somebody moving in the woods. Still, I was pretty happy, for I'd found it at last. Now I *knew* that the carpet factory was polluting the Timber River: that dead furrow beneath the pipe proved it as much as anything could.

What I needed to do now was to take some pictures of the pipe that I could show to the editor of the *Timber Falls Journal*. It would be best if I could get a picture when stuff was flowing out of the pipe. That might be pretty hard. I had a hunch that they dumped the stuff at night, when people were less likely to notice it. But maybe it would be enough to take a picture of the pipe with that furrow beneath it. It seemed pretty convincing to me. There was only one problem: I didn't have a camera, and I sure wasn't going to ask Dad to get one for me.

Suddenly I heard voices. I jumped. They were somewhere in the woods behind me. I couldn't make out the words. I leapt up and strained to listen. Someone was searching for me. It sounded like they were out by the road, a little downstream from me. My heart was racing and I began to sweat. Moving as quiet as I could, I slipped back into the middle of the woods, halfway between the river and the road, and headed farther upstream, to put whoever it was behind me. Every little bit and I'd stop to listen, and after a while I realized that the voices were gone.

What did that mean? Had they stopped talking, or had they gone away? I decided to slip carefully back to the road and see if anybody was out there. I went along with my body bent as low as I could, and after a bit I could see the road and the fields beyond it through the trees. I dropped to my knees, and crawled, swiveling my head left and right so as to catch a glimpse of anyone coming from either direction. Then I came to the edge of the woods, and stopped. There was nobody there. I stood up, and just at that moment the police car came sliding slowly by. The cop looked at me and I looked at the cop. There wasn't any hope of running or flinging the binoculars off into the woods. The car stopped instantly, and the cop at the wheel was out of it before I could move. The security guard got out the other side of the car.

SIX

"What're you doing here, son?" the cop said.

I knew him. He was the same guy who had come out to the house with Jim Otto that time that Dad stole the chain saw.

"I told you he had glasses," the security guard said. "He was spying."

The cop ignored him. "What's your name?"

It's a terrible thing to know that the minute somebody knows your name they'll think you're a thief. It made me feel hurt and sore and confused. I thought about giving the cop a false name, but I didn't dare. It would be worse if he caught me lying. I decided that at least I wouldn't be ashamed of it, and I looked the cop in the face and said, "My name's Harry White."

The cop squinted at me. "You one of the Whites out on Mountain Pass Road?"

"That's where I live," I said.

"Where'd you get the glasses?"

There was nothing to do but tell the truth. "My dad gave them to me."

"White," the security guard said. "I know who those people are. Stole the glasses, you can count on it."

The cop waved his hand at the security guard to shut him up. "You can't go accusing people of stealing without proof," he said. Then he turned back to me. "Sure your dad gave them to you?"

I was beginning to lose my temper, which I knew I shouldn't do. "He gave them to me," I said.

The cop looked at me some more. "What are you doing out here?"

"Looking for birds," I said. "Somebody said there was a pileated woodpecker down by the carpet factory. I was looking for it."

"The carpet factory's across the river," the security guard said.

"I didn't want to get too close and scare it. I figured I'd try to spot it from this side of the river." I didn't know if they believed me, but it was a good story.

The cop went on staring at me. Then he said, "Get in the car."

"I didn't—"

"Get in the car."

I got in the back and sat there, feeling scared and sore and confused all at once. I just sat there with my feelings going every which way, wondering what they were going to do with me when they got me down to the police station.

But the cop didn't start the car. Instead he began talking into the radio. "Eddie," he said, "have we got anything on a pair of binoculars?" He turned around to me. "Let me see 'em." I unslung the binoculars and gave them to him. "Pair of seven by thirty-fives. Look new."

The radio crackled and sputtered, and I sat there waiting and sweating under my jacket as if it was July and not April. Then the voice came back on: "Nothing. Nothing recent anyways."

I was so relieved, I almost grinned. But I kept my face still. "See, I told you," I said.

The cop swiveled around in the seat and stared me in the face. "Okay," he said. "But stay away from here. This is private property. Next time I'll take you in and book you for trespass. Understand?" He handed the binoculars back.

I jumped out of there as fast as I could, and started walking for home. So maybe Dad hadn't stolen the binoculars after all. He hadn't stolen them from the Sports Center, anyway, because Old Man Greenberg would have reported them missing. You had to do that to collect the insurance. And, too, most other people around Timber Falls would have reported it to the police if they were stolen.

Still, why had they come without a box and the instructions and all? That was hard to explain. Dad wouldn't have taken them out of the box and then thrown the box away. He would have brought them home in the box.

Then something else came to me. Maybe they weren't new. Maybe he had bought them second-hand. That would explain why they hadn't come in a box. So maybe he hadn't stole them after all.

Thinking that made me feel a whole lot better—not just about the binoculars but about everything. Suddenly I began to feel pretty cheerful. I had a terrific pair of binoculars, and I'd found that pipe. That was the great thing. I'd found the pipe, and now I knew for sure that the carpet factory was polluting the Timber River. There wasn't any doubt about that. For one thing, there was that furrow: weeds grow up awful quick, especially in the spring, and if they weren't spilling stuff into the river from that pipe down the bank, there'd be something growing there even in April. For another thing, it was plain as could be that upstream from the factory the water was clear, and downstream from it, it was tinged green, with oil slicks on the surface. The proof was all there.

But would people believe it? Would the newspaper people believe it if some kid, especially one everybody thought was trash, came in and said that the carpet factory was polluting the river? I wasn't sure. I needed more proof, and the obvious thing was to take some photographs. It wouldn't be hard to take pictures of the pipe during the day, if I was willing to chance going out there again. But the best thing would be to go out there some night and get some pictures when there was stuff actually pouring into the river. That would be proof nobody could deny. But I had no camera, and how was I going to get one?

That night, after supper, I went outside and sat on the back step to think about it. There weren't any stars out, or any moon, because it was so overcast. I remembered a song we had at school that went, "My

Lord, what a morning, when the stars begin to fall."
It was about Judgment Day, when the sinners would
be judged. I wondered if that was right, did the people who did wrong ever get punished, or did they go
on getting away with stuff forever?

I sat there thinking about things like that, listening
to the peepers and smelling the cool damp of the
spring night. The only light came from the kitchen
window. It fell on the lawn in a yellow square. There
was a little breeze, and I knew I would have to put on
a sweater if I was going to sit out there very long.

I couldn't ask Dad about a camera, that was for
sure. I didn't know how much it would cost to get a
camera with a flash attachment, but I'd seen some
advertised on TV for around thirty bucks or something. It was the same story as raising money for
binoculars. I'd have been glad enough to work to
earn the money, but there wasn't much work around
for kids. Work was so short around Timber Falls that
grown men got the odd jobs. If somebody needed the
snow shoveled out of his driveway, or his lawn cut, he
would hire a grown man. People felt they ought to
give the work to a man with a family to support. They
even had grown-ups packing bags at the checkout
counters at the supermarkets, where in other towns
they had kids. I knew because there was a story about
it in the paper.

So I couldn't buy a camera; and I wasn't about to
steal one, even if I had the nerve to try it. The only
thing left was to borrow one, and there was nobody I
could borrow anything from.

I was sitting there worrying about that when I heard a voice, just a quick whisper, say "Harry."

At least I thought I heard it. I've had that happen before, where you distinctly hear somebody call your name, and you look around and there's nobody there, and you realize you've been hearing things. So I figured that's what it was this time, because who could be around?

But then it came again: "Harry."

"Who's out there?" I said.

"Shss, shss" came out of the dark.

"Who's there?" I whispered.

"It's me," the whisper came back. "I'm up by the barn."

It was Helen. I jumped up, ran quickly up toward the barn, and stood by the barn door looking around. It was pretty dark, and I couldn't see her.

"I'm in here," she said. "Don't turn on the lights." Then I saw her, just a black shape edged up against the barn door. I slipped inside where nobody could see me from the house, and she threw her arms around my neck and kissed me.

"Where've you been?" I whispered.

"Shsss," she said. "Let's go up in the loft. We can turn on a light up there. You can't see it from the house."

She started to climb up the loft ladder, in the dark, and I started up behind her. She was carrying something. "What's that?" I said.

"New suitcase," she said.

We got into the loft and, feeling our way through the furniture and junk, moved down to the other

end. She turned on a little light she had rigged up
with an extension cord that ran through a crack in
the floor down to a plug below. She'd made a kind of
little room at this end of the loft, sort of a private
room where she could have guys over. I looked at
Helen. She'd changed. She was wearing her old
jeans, but she had on a fancy new pink blouse with a
lot of frills down the front, and she had a new black
purse hanging from her shoulder. She'd changed her
hair, too: Instead of just hanging down the way she
usually had it, it was piled up on top of her head. She
had on a lot of makeup, too—lipstick, and stuff on her
eyelashes and cheeks. She was different all right.

"Where've you been?" I said in a low voice, although I didn't think they could hear us in the house
anyway.

"New York City," she said. "I've been down in New
York City."

"I thought you might go there," I said. "Where are
you staying?"

"I've got a place to stay with some people," she
said. "Some other girls. Women, I guess."

"You mean they just let you live there?" I said.

"I pay rent." She seemed proud of that. "I'm earn-
ing money."

"You got a job?" I said.

"Yes," she said. She unslung her purse, snapped it
open, and held up a wad of bills. "Look," she said.

"Wow," I said. "What kind of job?"

"Just some kind of a job," she said.

"I mean in a store or something?"

"Here," she said. She took a hundred-dollar bill out of the stack and handed it to me. "Keep it," she said.

"A hundred dollars?" I said. "A hundred dollars?" I'd never had that much money in my life.

"Sure," she said. "Keep it. I've got plenty of money."

I wondered where she was getting all that money from. "Somebody at school heard you were dealing drugs."

"Oh, them," she said. "Those kids don't know anything. They don't know anything about New York. Why do I care what they think, Charlie Fritz and those guys. They're just a bunch of hicks."

"Are you sure you're not dealing drugs?" I said.

"Why should I deal drugs? I don't need to deal drugs. I've got plenty of money."

"You must have a pretty good job."

"Yeah," she said. Then she said, "Harry, you ought to see what it's like down there. There's anything you want there. You can go to the movies all the time and eat anything you want to eat. We're always going to the movies, these women I'm living with, and we don't bother to cook but eat out most of the time, or send out for stuff. If I want some beer or wine or something, they get it for me."

I decided I wouldn't ask her where she was getting the money from anymore. "How old are these women? Do they drink a lot?"

"They're in their twenties, I guess. They drink some, but mostly they get high. They get high all the time. I can, too, if I want. They don't mind giving me joints if I want to get high."

"Aren't you worried about the cops?"

"No," she said. "Down in New York the cops don't care what you do. Sometimes I can't believe it, being down there."

"Don't you miss home any? Don't you ever get homesick?"

She frowned. "Well, sometimes," she said. "The first couple of nights I was pretty homesick."

"Did you hitch down?"

"Yes," she said. "A guy picked me up and took me down to the thruway, and then I got a couple of rides to Albany and after that somebody took me to New York City."

"Weren't you scared riding with strange guys?"

"Yeah, sort of. The first guy kept reaching over to pat me on the leg or on my shoulder or something, and the guy that took me down to New York wanted me to go out to dinner with him and go to a nightclub and stuff, but I jumped out at a red light. I said, 'Thanks for the ride, I have to get off here,' and I jumped out. But I tell you, Harry, it didn't matter if I was scared, it didn't matter what those guys did to me, anything was worth it to get away from here." Suddenly she looked hard and angry. "I'm never coming back here as long as I live."

I didn't like to hear her say that. I would miss her a lot. "It isn't so bad here," I said.

"Yeah, sure," she said. "Yeah, sure. You know what they think about us in Timber Falls. They think we're nothing. They think we're the scum of the earth."

It was the first time she'd ever admitted it. "I used to tell you that," I said. "You would never believe it."

"Who would want to believe something like that?" She was still looking hard and sore. "Who would want to believe that your family is the scum of the earth? It's because of Mom and Dad. It's because Dad won't get a regular job and Mom wouldn't keep us clean and all that."

I decided I wouldn't say anything about Dad stealing. It would make her hate Timber Falls even more. "And having a junky house," I said, "with the paint peeling off and old cars in the yard."

"I'm never coming back," she said. "After this I'm never coming back."

"It's making Mom sad," I said.

"I don't care," she said. "I don't care if she dies of sadness. I don't care if they both die."

That kind of talk scared me a little. "You don't really want them to die, do you?"

"Yes, I do. Yes, I do." She put her hands over her face and started to cry, but then she stopped herself. "Listen, Harry, I came up to get my clothes and stuff. You have to help me get it. I'll pay you."

"You don't have to pay me. You already gave me a hundred dollars." I wondered why she came all the way home for those old clothes when she had all that money.

"That wasn't for anything," she said. "That was for nothing."

"How am I going to get your stuff out of there? I mean Mom will go up there and see everything gone."

"I'll be out of here by that time. The minute you get the stuff out, I'll pack it in the suitcase and go."

"Dad might not be around tomorrow," I said. "Sometimes he takes off on Sundays."

"We have to do it tonight," she said. "We have to wait until they're asleep. Then you can go into my room and throw the stuff out the window. I'll pack it up and hitch over to Watertown. I can get a bus there."

"I don't know if I can stay awake until they go to bed," I said.

"They don't stay up too late," she said. "You can have some coffee."

It worked out just the way she figured. I went back into the house, and upstairs, and opened Helen's window. Then I went downstairs and sat watching TV with Mom and Dad for a while. They stayed up for the news and then they went to bed. I went up and lay there on my bed for a while. After a little I shut off my light like I was going to sleep, and went on lying there in the dark with my clothes on. When I figured they were asleep, I tiptoed into Helen's room and looked out the open window. I could hardly see anything, but I could just make her out waiting out there. I threw her stuff down. There wasn't much of it: a pair of jeans, a couple of blouses, a sweater, some underwear, a pair of beat-up running shoes, and a pair of regular shoes. It wouldn't anyway near fill the suitcase she'd brought.

When I'd flung everything down, I decided to take a chance and go down to say good-bye. If Mom and Dad woke up, I'd say I thought I heard a raccoon trying to open the garbage cans. So I crept out of Helen's room, down the stairs, and out the kitchen door. Helen was around the side of the house jamming her stuff into the suitcase. She wasn't folding it or anything—just jamming it in. I knelt down and helped her, and then without saying anything, we went down the dirt driveway and out onto the road. We could hardly see each other. The peepers were still going and it was pretty chilly.

"You ought to put on your sweater," I said.

Suddenly she put her arms around me and squeezed me. "Sometimes I get so homesick. I keep on missing you, Harry."

"Maybe you ought to come back," I said.

"No," she said. "I'm never coming back. I get homesick sometimes, but I'm never coming back."

"There's nobody for me to talk to now," I said.

"I know," she said. She took her arms off me. "I didn't really come up to get those clothes," she said. "I just missed you. I came up to see if you were all right."

"I'm okay," I said.

"In three more years you'll graduate and you can leave too."

I didn't say anything. So she squeezed me again. "Well, I better get going." She turned and started walking off fast down the road. In a moment I couldn't see her anymore. I wondered when I would ever see her again.

SEVEN

It took Mom three or four days to realize that Helen's stuff was missing. I guess she was trying to stay away from Helen's room and forget about her, but one day, just as I was coming in through the kitchen door after school, she was coming down the stairs with a funny look on her face. "Harry, Helen's clothes are gone."

I tried to look surprised. "Gone?" I said.

"Yes, they're gone," she said. "You don't know what happened to them, do you?"

"I didn't do anything with them," I said.

"I know you didn't," she said. "You're a good boy, Harry." She stopped to think. "Maybe your dad packed them away."

But when he came home for supper, he was just as surprised as she was. He went upstairs and stood in the middle of Helen's room, looking around. There wasn't much to see—a few of her books under her bed, and some makeup on one of the windowsills.

"Nobody would have stolen the stuff," he said. "It wasn't worth stealing." He stood in the middle of the room scratching his head. "I'll bet she took her clothes herself. I'll bet she came up here some time when nobody was home and took them herself." He gave me a quick look. "You haven't seen her, have you, Harry?"

"No," I said.

He cocked his head and stared at me, but I managed to give him a straight look. "It had to be her," he said. "If anyone wanted to steal something from around here, they wouldn't have taken a few old clothes. They'd have taken the TV or some of the tools out of the barn. It had to be her."

"You mean she was here?" Mom said. "And she didn't want to see us?" She put her hands over her face and began to cry. It made me feel awful to see her cry like that, when I knew where Helen was.

"At least we know she's all right, Doris," Dad said.

Mom went on crying. "I don't care," she said. "I want my baby back. I miss her so much. I want her back."

"She's sixteen, Doris," Dad said. "She'd have left home in a couple of years anyway."

"Maybe she wouldn't have," Mom said. She tried to stop crying and it made her gasp. "Maybe she would have gone on living at home."

The whole thing seemed weird to me. How could Mom think Helen would want to go on living in some junky place like ours with a tough father who paid hardly any attention to anybody and a mom who spent all her time in a bathrobe watching TV? Didn't they know anything about us? But I didn't say anything.

"Doris, that's wishful thinking," Dad said. "Helen's pretty, she's bound to get married soon anyway. Maybe that's what happened. Maybe she and her boyfriend ran off to get married." He looked at me. "Who's her boyfriend, Harry?"

He'd already forgotten that I'd told him she didn't have a boyfriend. "I don't think she had a boyfriend," I said.

Mom shook her head. "Helen wasn't interested in boys," she said. She stopped crying and wiped her eyes on her bathrobe. "She told me so. Once I asked her if she had a boyfriend, and she said no, she wasn't interested in boys. Helen's young for her age. She's still my baby." She looked like she was going to start crying again, but she didn't.

Of course Helen had to tell Mom she wasn't interested in boys. How else could she explain why she didn't have a boyfriend? Could she tell Mom that she didn't have a boyfriend because all the boys thought she was trash? I couldn't stand thinking about it anymore, and I went out to the barn to see if I could get the lawnmower started. The grass was getting long and it was about time I started cutting it. It was always a problem getting the mower started the first time each spring.

The main thing was, now I had the hundred bucks that Helen had given me. That meant that I could buy some kind of camera to take photographs of that pipe with. For I was determined to go back there again, regardless of the risk. I would just be more careful this time.

The big problem was the hundred-dollar bill. If I tried to pay for the camera with a hundred-dollar bill, they were bound to think I'd stolen it. Any other kid could say he'd got it from his father, or his grandfather had given it to him for his birthday, or something, and they'd believe him.

Could I say that my sister had sneaked up from New York and had given it to me? No, I couldn't just spend the hundred-dollar bill the way anyone else could. I'd have to get it changed into fives and tens first, which wouldn't look so suspicious.

I wished I'd thought of it and asked Helen to give me tens instead of a hundred. But it was too late for that. The big question was, where to cash it?

In the end I had to ask Dad to change it. I hated to do it, because I knew what he would think. But I didn't have any choice. So one night at supper I said, "Dad, I found a hundred-dollar bill."

"What?" he said. "You found a hundred dollars?" He gave me a look. "Where?"

"On the street," I said. "In front of the bank. Somebody must have dropped it when they came out."

He squinted at me. "In front of the bank?"

"I want to change it, but I figure if I asked them to change it at the bank, they'd think I stole it or something."

"Found it?" he said. He gave me a grin. "Sure, you found it."

I expected that, but it made me mad anyway. "I didn't steal it," I said.

"Did I say you stole it?" he said.

I was feeling plenty hot. "You can't say I stole it."

"Frank, Harry wouldn't steal," Mom said. Then she looked at me. "You didn't steal it, did you, Harry?"

"I didn't steal it, everybody," I said.

"You see, Frank," Mom said. "He didn't steal it."

"Okay, he didn't steal it," Dad said. "Give it to me, and I'll cash it for you."

The truth was, I didn't want to give it to him. I didn't really trust him. I thought he might have a hundred dollars in his wallet and could change it right then. But I realized that he probably didn't have a hundred dollars on him very often. So I handed over the bill. He tucked it into his wallet, and the next day he brought me back the change in tens. He counted off ten ten-dollar bills, and then he took one off the top and put it into his pocket. "I figure anybody who is that rich can make a contribution to the household expenses," he said.

It made me good and mad, but I didn't dare say anything, for I knew that if I argued with him, he'd just take another ten to show me who was boss.

The next day after school I went to the drugstore and bought a camera. It was an Olympus with a built-in flash and timer so you could take pictures of yourself. I bought a lot of color film, and extra batteries, and a case for it. The whole thing cost fifty-five dollars. It was a lot of money, but at least I was getting something for it.

It felt really good to have my own camera. I took it home, put it down on the kitchen table, and sat there staring at it. I really loved looking at it. I loved looking at the dials and the various buttons and knobs for switching on the flash or the timer, so you could take a picture of yourself. I figured I'd do that; I figured if nobody else would take the pictures of me when something interesting was happening, I'd take them myself. I just wished Helen was back. I could have taken a lot of pictures of her. She would have liked that.

Mom came out into the kitchen and saw the camera. "Oh, my," she said. "What a fancy camera. How much did it cost?"

I told her.

"My goodness," she said. Then she looked at me. "Harry, you didn't steal that money, did you?"

"Mom, I didn't steal it."

"Honestly?"

"I swear it, Mom."

"You've always been a good boy," she said.

"I wouldn't steal anything," I said. I hoped that was true. It still worried me that maybe someday I would.

She sighed. "I wonder if you should have returned the money."

"Returned it? Who would I return it to?"

"Why, the bank."

She was right, of course. If I'd really found it the way I'd said, I probably would have taken it into the bank and asked if they knew who'd lost it. But, of course, I hadn't found it—Helen had given it to me. "How would they know who lost it?"

She sighed again. "Yes, I suppose that's right. You deserve it, Harry."

I didn't know if I did. But I was going to keep it. To

change the subject, I told Mom I would take some pictures of her, to try out the camera. She made me wait until she put on a dress instead of her bathrobe and combed her hair. She kept fussing and fidgeting like she'd never had her picture taken before. To tell the truth, I guess it had been a long time since she'd had her picture taken. The only pictures of her that I'd ever seen were the one of her holding me when I was a baby, and a couple that she and Dad had taken on their wedding day, which were in a double frame on the dresser in their bedroom. They were just pictures of Mom and Dad, looking young, standing with their arms around each other in front of an old brick building in Watertown—the courthouse, or the justice of the peace's office, or something. So I took some pictures of her, and when she discovered about the self-timer, she had me take some pictures of the two of us standing there together.

After I'd taken a bunch of pictures of Mom, I went outside and took some more, some with the flash and some without. And that night, after it was good and dark, I walked down the dirt driveway until I was a good way from the barn—about as far as I figured I'd be from the pipe when I was photographing it—and took some flash pictures. I shot up the whole two rolls on these various tests, and the next day I took them into the drugstore to get them developed. They came back the next Monday. They were pretty good, and I was satisfied that I'd be able to get good pictures.

Mom was tickled over the shots I'd made of her. When she dressed up and combed her hair, and smiled the way she did for the camera, she really looked pretty. At supper she showed them to Dad. He said it was a lot of middle-class baloney, but a couple of days later I noticed that he'd got one of them taped up in the cab of the truck. And later, when I got to meet my grandparents for the first time, I saw sitting on their mantelpiece in a little frame a picture of me and Mom standing side by side. Mom had sent it to them that Christmas. But that was later.

Now I was all set, and I was pretty nervous. If they caught me out there again, they were sure to know that I wasn't watching any birds, I was up to something. I was bound to get into serious trouble with the police. It wouldn't be just trespassing; they'd figure out something worse to charge me with.

But going out there at night would be an advantage. For one thing, the security guard wouldn't be able to see me—at least not until I fired off the flash. For another, if anyone did come after me, they'd have an awful hard time finding me in the dark woods. Somehow, I could manage to lose them and escape. There was an awful lot of woods in the Adirondacks to hide in.

It rained the whole next weekend. I hadn't been able to get the lawnmower started before, so I spent most of the weekend working on it. Because of the rain Dad was around a lot, and I knew he could get it started easy. He liked fooling around with engines, and he could usually get them to work. But I didn't want to be around him anymore. I didn't like the feeling of having him near me, his old work shirt and jeans, and the stubble on his face from not shaving. Once during the weekend he came out and stood there watching me strip the engine down. "Want some help?" he said.

"No," I said, not looking up. "I can do it myself." And I did. Once I got the jets cleaned out, and the air filter washed, and cleaned off the spark plug and put in fresh gas, it started. I was proud of myself, even if it had taken most of the weekend to do it.

All the next week I kept watching the weather report on TV, and by Thursday I knew it was going to be a good weekend—sunny and seasonable weather, the way they say. I didn't care how warm it was, so long as it wasn't raining and the woods were dry. I knew I might have to sit out there with the camera for a while, and I didn't want to get soaked and start sneezing, or something.

It turned out to be a perfect day for cutting wood too. Dad had an order for a couple of cords, which would pay a hundred dollars. Whenever we got an order for cordwood, we went up into the woods that sloped up toward the mountains behind the house. It wasn't our land—we just rented the house—and we weren't supposed to cut wood there, but we always did. Dad was careful just to cut here and there so we wouldn't make a big clearing that would be obvious. He cut low to the ground, so that the stumps were practically flat, and if you kicked a little dirt over them, you wouldn't notice them unless you were looking for them. We mostly cut dead stuff, anyway, which burned easier. The people we rented from didn't come around much. Dad said they were afraid to because he might demand they fix up the house. I knew that wasn't it, though, because once Helen, after she got interested in guys, asked Mom why the people wouldn't fix up the house a little. Mom said it was because we paid such a low rent, Dad couldn't ask them to do anything to the house.

So we took Dad's old chain saw up into the woods and cut. Dad ran the chain saw, and I trimmed the branches off the logs and scattered the brush around the woods so it wouldn't be in a noticeable pile. In a couple of years it would begin to rot away. We worked all morning and into the afternoon, and then we drove the truck up into the woods as far as it would go, loaded it up, and drove around to the people who had ordered the wood.

It was a big house, one of these old farmhouses that somebody had spent a lot of money fixing up. It was white clapboard with big maple trees and a lot of lawn around it. A bluestone driveway circled around to the back. There was a new-painted red barn here, and some nicely pruned apple trees beside the barn. A Mercedes was parked on the bluestone. It was some place all right. I wondered what it would be like to have all that money and be able to have everything you wanted. Would I ever have that much money? I didn't think so; I didn't think you got paid a whole lot in the air force—just a good salary. It kind of hurt to know that I'd never be rich. Dad always said that money corrupted people, and he wished he was corrupted. I didn't know if it did or it didn't, but I sure wished I had money.

We crunched over the bluestone and stopped behind the house. A man came out of the kitchen door and started walking toward the truck. He was wearing blue jeans with a crease in them and a bright red flannel shirt and shiny loafers.

"That's Herbst," Dad said in a low voice. "He's one of the biggies at the carpet factory. House cost a half million dollars to do over. They practically had to rebuild it. You don't get that kind of money running a chain saw. You squeeze it out of the working people."

Mr. Herbst came up to the truck, and Dad and I got out. Dad spit on the bluestone. It was his way of showing Mr. Herbst that he was as good as Mr. Herbst was, and wasn't going to take anything from him.

Mr. Herbst looked at the wood. "Is it good and dry?"

I knew it wasn't, but Dad didn't lie about it. "Mixed," he said. "Some dry and some green. You want a mix. Green burns hotter and slower." He spit again.

Mr. Herbst didn't say anything but turned and started to walk back to the house. "I want it in the basement," he said. "I'll show you where."

We followed him into the house through the kitchen door. I'd never seen such a kitchen in my life. It was gleaming and bright and spotless, and it had everything you could want—a fancy stove, a wall oven, a dishwasher, a garbage compactor, a microwave oven, and other stuff I couldn't figure out. It was some kitchen.

The cellar door was across the kitchen from the back door. They'd laid newspapers on the floor tiles so we wouldn't mess the floor when we carried the wood in. "This your boy, Frank?" Herbst said.

"He's my boy," Dad said.

Mr. Herbst looked at me. "You go to school, son?"

"Yes," I said. "I'm in ninth grade." It felt pretty funny to me to be talking to one of the biggies from the carpet factory, knowing that pretty soon I was going to go out there and catch them polluting the river. It didn't scare me exactly; it just felt funny.

He stared at me. "The police picked up a kid with a pair of binoculars out at the plant a couple of weeks ago," he said. "That wasn't you, was it?"

I was shocked that he knew about it, and I flashed hot. There wasn't any use in lying about it, though. "I was looking for birds," I said.

"What's this?" Dad said. "You didn't tell me you got picked up by the cops."

He didn't really care if I got picked up by the cops. He was just acting that way so he would look like a good father.

"It wasn't anything," I said. "I was looking for a pileated woodpecker that somebody said was in there, and the cops wanted to know what I was doing. They thought I stole the binoculars." The minute I said that I wished I hadn't.

"Who said you stole them?" Dad said. "Nobody's going to make accusations like that to me. I'm not going to put up with it."

"It wasn't anything, Dad," I said. "They checked and found out they weren't stolen."

Dad's jaw was jutting out. "They better have," he said.

Mr. Herbst didn't say anything; he just stood there listening, and I was embarrassed to have this conversation in front of him. Finally he said, "You'll see where the wood is stacked. There's beer in the refrigerator when you're finished." Then he went out of the kitchen through a swinging door.

EIGHT

That night I sat on the back steps, watched the stars come out—and I thought about it. It seemed strange to me that Mr. Herbst had known about me getting picked up by the cops out by the carpet factory. He was one of the biggies there: why would they have bothered him about finding some kid in the woods looking for birds? They wouldn't have, unless they believed there was more to it—unless they were suspicious and had guessed that I wasn't really looking for birds. That worried me a good deal because it gave me the idea that they didn't really believe my story. What were they thinking? Who actually knew about the pollution pipe?

I didn't think that most of the people who worked at the carpet factory would know about it. If they did, somebody would have been bound to report it to the police, or tell the editors of the *Journal*. But a few of them had to know about it. Whoever it was who turned the valve had to know about it, and probably several people were in on that. Then the security guards had to know about it. I didn't know how many security guards they had, but if they only had one on duty at a time, each guard working an eight-hour shift, that made three; and it seemed likely to me that there would be more than one on duty during the daytime, when they had to have somebody on the gate. And, of course, at least some of the biggies knew about it. When you added it up, it seemed like at least a dozen people must have known about that pollution pipe. So it wasn't any big secret, and why would they worry about me finding out?

But maybe I was wrong about it. Maybe the security guard was the one who turned the valve to let the chemicals run into the river. Maybe the only people who knew about it were the guard himself and one of the biggies like Mr. Herbst. *He* knew about it, that was plain, because the security guard had told him about me being out there with binoculars, and they wouldn't have told him if they hadn't been worried about me spotting that pipe.

The only thing that was clear about it was, they didn't want anybody spotting that pipe. It was chancy for them, I figured, because they could never tell when a hunter might be out there; or somebody looking for birds; or some people just having a walk in the woods after Sunday dinner. Anybody could spot that pipe by chance, and they had to be worried about that. And I guessed that was why the security guard told Mr. Herbst that he had caught me out there. Even if it had been true that I was only a kid looking for birds, they had to be worried that I had seen that pipe and might report it.

Did they believe my story? I figured they probably did: why would they suspect some ninth-grade kid of going out there to look for that pipe? But if they caught me out there again, especially at night with a camera, I could lie until I was blue in the face, and they wouldn't believe me. Then what would they do? They would want to keep me quiet, that was sure, and how would they go about that? They'd be sure to press some kind of charges against me so as to get me sent away to a place for juvenile offenders.

I was beginning to feel like maybe I ought to forget about the whole thing. If something went wrong, I was going to be in an awful lot of trouble. Once I'd been convicted of a crime, I'd never get into the air force. There wouldn't be a chance of that. There wouldn't be any chance of getting respected around Timber Falls after that either. Having Helen run off hadn't helped improve our reputation. It didn't matter that she had good reason to run off, and it didn't matter where she was, and what she was doing. They all believed that she had run off to do something bad, and *was* doing something bad.

So there were a lot of good reasons for giving the whole thing up. But I didn't want to do it. There was something stubborn in me that wouldn't let me quit. I wanted to do it, and I was going to take the chance.

The real danger would be in shooting off the flash camera. I'd be safe enough going out there at night. There was never much traffic on that beat-up blacktop road. Anyway, I could spot the headlights of a car coming along, long before they would see me, and I could duck into the woods until it went past. So I'd be safe enough getting out there; and once I got into the woods, I'd be safe enough there.

But the minute I shot off the flashgun they'd know it. Well, there would always be the hope that the security guard would be around the other side of the factory when I shot the camera off, and wouldn't see the flash, but I couldn't take a chance on that. The minute I shot the flash off I would have to run for it. It would take ten minutes for the security guard or the cops or anybody to get out there, and in ten minutes I could run a mile on up the road and hide in the woods. There wasn't any way you could find somebody in the woods, especially at night, unless you tracked them with dogs, and I didn't think the Timber Falls cops had dogs. There was another bridge across the river two or three miles farther upstream. I could make my way up there, and be home in half an hour. If worst came to worst, I could swim across the river and go home cross-country through the woods. It wouldn't be much fun hiking home through the woods wet, but it would be safe. There were an awful lot of woods around there for them to search through.

So that was the plan. I waited a couple of days to give myself time to see if there were any flaws in it. I couldn't find any, so on Wednesday, after supper, I sneaked the camera and the binoculars out into the yard and hid them under a bush. Then I swiped Dad's flashlight out of the truck. It was a big one, the kind that takes four batteries, and had a powerful beam. I wondered if he had stolen it. Suppose they found out that the binoculars were stolen after all, and the flashlight, too—they'd put me down for a thief in a minute, and send me away. It was the chance I'd have to take.

I hid the flashlight under the bush, with the camera and binoculars. The stars were bright; it was going to be another clear night. I went into the house and watched TV with Mom and Dad to stay awake. They went to bed after the ten o'clock news. I went upstairs, too, got under the blankets with my clothes on and my shoes off, and waited until I figured they were asleep. Then I picked up my shoes, slipped down the stairs in my stocking feet and out the kitchen door. I sat down on the back step, put my shoes on, and then collected the stuff I'd hidden under the bush. I stuck the flashlight through my belt, slung the binoculars around my neck, and buttoned them and the camera under my jacket. Then I took off, jogging for a hundred yards, then walking for a while, and then jogging again. The moon was just beginning to come up through the trees.

There weren't many cars out. I didn't need to hide yet, so when I saw one coming, I would stop jogging and just walk casually along like some kid on the way home. Finally I got to town. I went through as quickly as I could without looking suspicious. If a cop who knew who I was spotted me, he was bound to ask me where I was going, and I'd have to lie and go home.

But nobody bothered me, and in a couple of minutes I was out of the town and across the steel bridge.

I went along the beat-up blacktop road that led out to where the pollution pipe was. Now I would have to be more careful; but no cars came along, and in a little while I turned off the road, into the woods.

The moon was up, and it was about as bright a night as it could be. In the open you could easily see a person fifty yards away. If anybody was watching, they'd have seen me slip into the woods, for sure. In the woods it was darker, and I couldn't see the brush underfoot very well. But the tree trunks were clear enough, and I was able to move along at a pretty good pace. It would have helped to use the flashlight, but of course I didn't dare. You could spot a light moving through the woods a long way off.

In a bit I began to hear the river rustling along through its banks. I slowed down and went forward easy and quiet as I could, and soon I could see the long white shine of moonlight glinting on the water. I dropped flat, crawled forward until I was right at the edge of the riverbank, and lay there staring out across the river.

The carpet factory was about fifty yards farther upstream from where I was. I didn't have any trouble seeing it: spotlights on the corners of the building were shining down into the parking lot, and there were more lights on posts at various places in the parking lot. Only a couple of cars were in the lot, and some trucks had been pulled up to the loading docks. I didn't see any people—no security guard or anyone else.

I pulled back into the woods and made my way upstream past the factory building, until I was opposite the point where I figured the pipe stuck out of the riverbank. I dropped down, crawled forward to the edge of the bank, and lay there looking out. The moon on the river was almost as bright as day, and I could see it flash and shine as the water rippled along. But the opposite bank was a different story. The moonlight fell on the bank at an angle, and it was hard to make out anything on it. It looked like patches and scraps of light and dark. I could hardly make out the shape of anything.

I saw right away the mistake in my plan. Unless I managed to spot the pipe, I would have to use my flashlight, and that would give me away. I wished I'd had sense enough to make some kind of mark on a tree or something, to show where the pipe was. Or maybe memorized something on the opposite bank just above the pipe, like a tree with a crooked branch or a fork. But it was too late for that.

I lay there staring across, tipping my head this way and that way, hoping to catch a glimpse of that straight black edge that would tell me where the pipe was. But I didn't see anything.

Maybe I was in the wrong place. Maybe the pipe was a little farther upstream or farther down. I slid back from the riverbank, went along a little bit, and took another look. I moved my eyes carefully along the bank, turning my head slowly. Still nothing. So I moved back down in the other direction, hoping that if I got a different angle on it I'd spot it. But I didn't.

Now what? I pulled the flashlight out of my belt and held it in my hand. It was a powerful light, so I was sure I'd be able to find the pipe pretty easily if I used it. But it would be pointing directly at the carpet factory, and there was no way that the security guard could miss it. Suppose it took a little while to find the pipe. Every minute it took would cut into my escape time.

I thought for a minute. One thing I could do would be to go home, come back again in the daylight, and mark the spot where the pipe was. Then I'd have to come back again another night to take the picture. The whole idea of that made me feel sick, for it meant coming out here twice more, and the risk of getting caught was a lot more. No, I'd better get the whole thing done now.

Then another idea came to me. I was bound to hear the noise when the pollution came splashing out. At least it seemed to me that I would, even over the rustling of the river. That would tell me where the pipe was, and I could take a couple of quick shots with the camera and make a run for it. It would be better that way because it would give me positive proof that they were dumping chemicals into the river.

So I sat there near the riverbank, listening to the noises of the night—the river sound and the peepers, and once a car going along the road. After a while I realized that I had dozed off. I rubbed my eyes and yawned, and shook my head to get the sleepiness out of it, and for a moment I felt wide awake. Then I started to doze again. I shook myself awake once more, but I knew that sooner or later I would fall asleep.

That was no good because I might be sound asleep

when the stuff poured out into the river. Now what? Either I had to forget about the whole thing and go home, or I had to take a chance. If I found the pipe right away, I'd be all right. I sat there thinking, and trying to get my nerve up. Finally I got up on my knees, set the flash on the camera, and laid it on the ground right in front of me where I'd be able to grab it in a hurry. Then I raised up the flashlight to point it out to about where I thought the pipe might be, took a deep breath, and turned it on.

The beam hit the opposite bank. No pipe. I moved it quickly left and right. Still no pipe. I swung it farther upstream, darting it back and forth along the bank, but now it was at a sharp angle and making a lot of shadows dance and leap around as I moved it. I'd never see the pipe among those shadows even if it was there. I stood up, and just then I heard the sound of a car starting by the carpet factory, and in ten seconds a Jeep came racing across the empty parking lot toward the riverbank. I grabbed up the camera and began to work my way through the trees as fast as I could move, tripping on the underbrush and bumping into things. When I'd made fifty feet, I snapped the flashlight on again and beamed it across the river. Still no pipe. I snapped the flashlight off, and then a spotlight from the Jeep hit the trees over my head. I was making a mess of the whole thing, and I knew I ought to forget about the pipe and make a run for it. There was bound to be a radio in the Jeep, and for sure the security guard had already called the police.

I ducked back into the woods. "Hey you," a voice

shouted. I looked across. The security guard was standing beside the Jeep, working the spotlight through the woods a little upstream from me. His other hand was on the butt of the pistol in his holster. As the light came around to point directly at me, everything disappeared into a great shining haze. I put my head down to get the light out of my eyes and prayed that he wouldn't see me.

Now what? Should I run for it? Where was that pipe? Was it back down the river in the other direction? What should I do? Across the river the man was shouting again. "Come on out of there, you. Come on out onto the bank where I can see you."

Cold sweat was dripping down my face. Keeping low, I began to work my way through the woods back downstream, until I was below the place where I had first turned on the flashlight. I wondered if the security guard would take a shot at me when I turned on the flashlight. I snapped on the light, and the beam hit the opposite bank. There was the pipe, and flowing out of it was a steady stream of liquid that shone green in the light. I hadn't been able to hear it after all. The guard shouted again, and the spotlight from the Jeep began to swing along toward me. I dropped flat, to be low in case he took a shot at me. Then I raised up the flash camera, sighted at where I'd seen the pipe, and fired it. The spotlight fell on me, and if the guard wanted to shoot me, he had a pretty good target. I shone the flashlight across the river again to make sure the pipe was there, rewound the camera, and fired it again. Then I grabbed up the flashlight and ran through the woods as fast as I could, banging into things, stumbling, and falling. In a minute I burst out onto the road, and here came the police cars, two of them, their spotlights shining into the woods as they came.

NINE

They told me to get in, and they took me down to the police station. The police station wasn't much. It was just a couple of rooms in the back of the old redbrick town hall. There were two cells behind the rooms. I knew because our class had gone there once when we'd had a tour of the town for social studies. I wondered if they were going to lock me in one of the cells.

They took me inside the station. There wasn't much to see. A fat cop who usually directed traffic at the school in the mornings was sitting behind a desk covered with papers. A radio sat on a table near to him. On one wall was a long bench, and on the opposite wall, a small table with a coffeepot on it, cups, a container of milk, and a box of doughnuts. Those doughnuts looked mighty good to me.

The cops who brought me in made me sit down on the bench, and then they went outside again. The fat cop at the desk didn't even look at me. I just sat there alone, feeling lousy—not scared so much as just low as could be. Everything was finished and done with. They would call my dad, that was for sure, and he was bound to belt me a few times for getting him into trouble with the cops.

Oh, how I wished I'd never started the whole thing. Oh, how I wished I'd minded my own business and put up with being trash and gone along until I graduated and could get into the air force. Why had I started this crazy thing? Why hadn't I had more sense?

But what had I really done wrong? Was there anything wrong with trying to catch the factory polluting the Timber River? That was against the law. Was there anything wrong with trying to stop people from breaking the law? Sure, I'd trespassed. That was true. But around Timber Falls everybody trespassed all the time. Outside of town there was nothing but woods and fields and mountains, and nobody knew who most of it belonged to, and nobody cared. They fished and hunted and went on picnics and walks wherever they wanted to go, and nobody paid any attention. Around there trespassing was hardly a crime. So what had I done wrong? Nothing, really. I was going to end up being convicted of stealing mainly because my name was White.

I began to get mad. It wasn't right and it wasn't fair. I thought about standing up and telling the fat cop at the desk that I hadn't done anything and they couldn't keep me there. But I decided I'd better not make things worse, so I just sat there and waited to see what would happen.

Ten minutes went by and then twenty. I was surprised. It wouldn't have taken Dad that long to come
down there. But he didn't come; I was trying to figure out why, when the door opened and Mr. Herbst
came in. That was a shock all right. He was wearing
his creased jeans and loafers and a fancy heavy
sweater that buttoned up the front. The cops who
had picked me up came in behind him. He looked
like he'd got out of bed and dressed in a hurry. He
stood in the middle of the room looking at me for a
minute. Then he turned to one of the cops. "Where'd
you actually find him?" Mr. Herbst said.

"We picked him up just as he was coming out of the
woods."

"The same place?"

"No," the cop said. "Maybe a mile further back
downstream toward town."

Mr. Herbst put his thumbs in his belt and looked at
me for a while. The cops didn't say anything but
waited for him to talk. It was clear enough that he
was the boss there, not the cops, and he'd decide
what was to be done with me. "Okay, Harry," he said
finally. "What's this all about?"

"I was looking for birds," I said.

"In the middle of the night?"

"Owls," I said. "I was trying to photograph owls."

He stared at me for a minute more, trying to decide what to believe. Then he said, "What gave you
the idea that there are owls in there?"

"I know they're there," I said. "When I was there
before, I saw owl pellets."

Mr. Herbst looked at one of the cops. "I don't know anything about birds," he said. "Is that reasonable?"

The cop shrugged. "Could be. They have a bird club at school. Sometimes you see them along the roads with their field glasses."

Mr. Herbst looked back at me. "You belong to the bird club, Harry?"

It made me blush to think about that, I don't know why. "No," I said. "I just study birds on my own."

He stared me right in the face in that way he had, thinking. Finally he said, "Did you see any owls?"

"I think so," I said.

"You can see in the dark?"

"On a bright night like this you can. They're light-colored. That's why I came out tonight, because it's so bright."

"And you took a picture of it?"

"I hope so," I said. "I tried, anyway."

He reached out his hand. "Mind if I have a look at the camera?"

I didn't want to give it to him. I was suspicious of him. "I—"

But the cop shook a finger at me. "Give it to him, White." I handed it over.

He looked it over for a minute. "Brand-new," he said.

"The kid's got a lot of new stuff," the cop said. "Binoculars, big flashlight."

I was beginning to lose my temper. "I bought that camera," I said. "It's mine."

"Don't get smart, White," the cop said. "Where'd you get it?"

"It's mine," I said. "I bought it at the drugstore. I have a receipt."

"Where'd you get the money?"

I knew I ought to be polite and not make everything worse, but I couldn't help myself. "I don't have to tell you that," I said. "It's none of your business."

"Don't worry, White," the cop said. "We can find out."

Mr. Herbst hadn't been paying any attention but had been turning the camera over in his hands, examining it. Then he put the camera into the pocket of his jacket and said, "Let him go." That was all; nothing more. But I knew what he was going to do. He was going to develop the film to see what I had been taking pictures of.

"Hey," I said. "That's my camera. You can't take that."

"Don't worry, Harry. You'll get it back. I'm just going to borrow it for a few days."

"Hey, wait a minute," I said. But he turned and walked out of the police station. "Hey," I said to the cop. "That's my camera. He can't take it like that."

"He's just borrowing it, White," the cop said. "Now you better get out of here before you get into real trouble. You're lucky you got let off. We could have booked you for a dozen things. Now scram on home."

There wasn't anything I could do about it, and so I left, feeling sore and scared and pretty mixed-up. It wasn't right for them to take my camera, and it wasn't right for them to treat me the way they did. They were the ones who were breaking the law, not me; but still, somehow I felt that everything was all my fault, that I was some kind of a criminal. The only luck I had was that Mom and Dad didn't hear me come home.

I woke up late the next morning. I realized right away that I'd missed the school bus. Dad was already gone, and Mom had forgotten I was there. When I came down, she said, "Oh, dear, I didn't realize you were still here. I thought you'd gone."

I didn't want to go to school. Everything from last night was still bothering me too much. "I don't feel good," I said.

She put her hand on my forehead. "You aren't hot," she said.

"I feel like I'm getting a cold," I said. "I think I'll stay home." I ate two peanut butter sandwiches on toast, which was all there was for breakfast, and then I went upstairs and lay on my bed and thought.

The whole thing had come to nothing. Mr. Herbst had the film and my camera. I figured he'd give the camera back, but he sure wouldn't give the film back. He would burn it, and there would go my proof. I couldn't possibly dare to go back out to the carpet factory to take more pictures. If I got caught out there one more time, they were bound to do something to me. I didn't know what, but something.

Why hadn't they arrested me last night? Why hadn't they charged me? The answer was pretty clear. If they took me to court, it was bound to come out about the way the factory was polluting the river. So Mr. Herbst didn't want to make a fuss over it. He just wanted to keep the whole thing quiet. He would destroy the film, and give me my camera back so I wouldn't make a fuss about that either. And that would be the end of the whole thing.

I didn't see how I could stand three more years of high school—three more years of no friends, and nobody talking to me except to say something snotty about Helen; three more years of knowing that everybody was looking down on me, of knowing that when I went into a store the owners were particularly keeping an eye on me all the time I was in there. And now Helen was gone, and I didn't even have her to talk to. I missed her all right.

I wondered where she was and what she was doing. I hoped she wasn't getting into some kind of trouble. All that money she had, had made me pretty suspicious. I just hoped she wasn't dealing drugs. She could get into bad trouble for that.

I went along for three or four days to make myself forget it, and then one day when I was coming out of school and heading across the parking lot to get on the bus, a big Mercedes pulled up beside me. Mr. Herbst was driving. He opened the door on the passenger side. "Get in," he said. He was used to giving orders, I could tell. The way he did it you just automatically did what he told you. So I got in and slammed the door. When I looked out the side window, there was a bunch of kids staring at me. They were pretty surprised to see trash like me getting into a car like that. I didn't want to smile, because I wanted them to think it was a normal thing for me, but I couldn't help it.

Mr. Herbst pulled out of the parking lot. "I think we need to have a talk, Harry," he said. "Let's go

down to my office where we won't be interrupted."
He drove through town and out along the road to the
carpet factory. All the way he asked me questions
about myself—how I was doing in school, what my
hobbies were—and about our family and so forth. I
didn't trust him and I didn't tell him any more than I
had to, and finally we got to the carpet factory. He
pulled into a parking space by the front door that had
a little sign on it saying MR. HERBST. We got out, and I
followed him into the front corridor past a desk
where a receptionist sat answering the phone. Down
at the end of the corridor there was a door with a
glass panel in it. On the door was lettered FREDERICK
J. HERBST, PRESIDENT. He was a biggie all right, and I
was going to talk to him in his office. The whole thing
puzzled me.

We went into the office. There was a big desk, a
sofa, a big glass table with fancy magazines lying on
it, a bookcase full of books, a thick blue carpet on the
floor, and a couple of easy chairs. It was more like a
living room than an office. I wondered if presidents
of companies always had offices like that.

Mr. Herbst sat down behind the desk and told me
to sit in one of the chairs. Then he leaned back in his
chair with his hands behind his head and stared at me
for a while. He did a lot of staring at people. I figured
he did it to worry you. Finally he said, "I got that film
developed, Harry. You weren't taking pictures of
owls."

I didn't say anything. There wasn't anything I
could say.

"Who put you up to this?" he said.

"Nobody," I said. "I did it on my own."

He shook his head. "No, you didn't, Harry. No high school kid is going to start an investigation like this on his own."

"Nobody put me up to it," I said. I didn't like being called a liar, and I was starting to get sore. "It was my own idea."

He sat there with his hands behind his head staring at me for a while. Then he said, "Harry, you'd better tell me the truth. I can make life pretty tough for you. I have a lot of power in this town. If I tell those cops I want you booked, they'll book you. We'll get you for something. Trespassing, malicious mischief—something. We'll put you down as incorrigible and send you off to a juvenile home for a couple of years. That'll be on your record for the rest of your life."

I didn't know if he really could do it, or was just bluffing, but it scared me plenty anyway. "I told you the truth," I said. "I can't help it if you won't believe me."

He took his hands from behind his head, put them on the desk, and leaned forward, watching my face. "Did your dad put you up to it? Was it that?"

"Dad doesn't know anything about it," I said.

"Is he trying to blackmail me? Is that his game?"

"I told you, I did it on my own. Dad doesn't know anything about it."

"Harry, I've tried to be easy with you, but if you go on lying to me, I'm going to have to get tough."

"I'm not lying," I said.

"Yes, you are," he said.

I jumped up. "Don't call me a liar," I shouted. "I

never did anything wrong. You're the one who's doing wrong. You're dumping stuff into the Timber River. I saw that stuff coming out of that pipe. You're the one who's doing wrong, not me."

He leaned back in his chair again. "Okay," he said. "Calm down. Let's try to keep it on a friendly basis." He reached into a drawer and took out my camera. "Here's your camera." He slid it across the desk, and I picked it up and stuck it in my jacket pocket. He took his wallet out. "I owe you for a roll of film," he said. "Is ten bucks enough?"

"It was only three-fifty."

He handed me the ten across the desk. "Keep it," he said. "Call it even for the loan of the camera."

I didn't want to take the extra money, but I didn't have any change, so I put the ten in my pocket. Then he picked up his phone, pressed a button, and said, "Get a driver to take Harry White home." He got up, came around from behind his desk, and shook my hand. I didn't want to do that, either, but there wasn't any way out of it. "No hard feelings," he said. "We'll talk about it some other time. I sympathize with your viewpoint, but you've got to understand ours too." He let go of my hand. "Go out to the receptionist. Somebody will take you home. And when you see your dad tonight, ask him to give me a call."

TEN

I hated being pushed around that way. I hated being called a liar. I hated having him threaten to put me in jail and all the rest of it. He was the one who was breaking the law, not me. I'd seen that green stuff coming out of that pipe, even if I didn't have the pictures to prove it. I was a witness. And I knew where the pipe was—I wouldn't have any trouble finding it now. Suppose I went down to the newspaper and told them what I knew. They were bound to run a story about it, and then people in Albany would hear about it and send somebody out to investigate. I could show them where the pipe was, and in the end the people from Albany would make them stop the pollution. It might work after all. But should I do it? Maybe it would just get me in more trouble. Maybe I ought to forget the whole thing and just sweat out three more years of being trash. The more trouble I got into, the more I was likely to ruin my chances of getting into the air force.

That night, when Dad came in, I told him that Mr. Herbst wanted him to call. I didn't say anything about going to his office or any of that. I just said that I'd bumped into him on the street after school.

Dad said, "I don't like working for that rich slicker. He's too smooth for me, with those two-hundred-dollar shoes and those hundred-dollar shirts. What did he want?"

"I don't know," I said. "Do his shoes really cost two hundred dollars?"

"What difference does it make to him what they cost?" Dad said. "He's taking the money out of the hides of working people anyway."

"Do you work for Mr. Herbst a lot?" I said.

Dad shrugged. "I got to make a living," he said. He sat down and began taking off his shoes.

"I didn't mean that," he said. "I just wondered if you knew him."

"Yeah, I know him," Dad said. "I wouldn't trust him as far as I could throw him. He's slick."

For the first time I began to think that maybe there was something to what Dad always said about the biggies taking it out of the hides of the workingman. Herbst was doing something wrong, and he was going to a lot of trouble to cover it up. That didn't exactly mean that he was taking it out of anybody's hide, except the ones who wanted to fish in the Timber River. But it did seem like he didn't mind breaking the law and lying about it. Would he ever get caught? When the stars began to fall would the sinners really be judged?

For a couple of days I thought about it. Was there

any way Herbst could get me into trouble if I went to the editors of the *Timber Falls Journal* and told them what I'd seen? Could he go back now and get me for trespassing or something, or was it too late? He had a lot of power in town, he said, and I knew he was right, from the way the cops had let him decide what to do about me—letting him take my camera, which he had no right to, and all that. But what could he actually do to me?

I couldn't figure it out, but it worried me, and I kept wondering if I ought to drop the whole thing. For a while I thought about sending the newspaper an anonymous letter. There wouldn't be much use in that, though. In the first place, they wouldn't know who it was who could show them where the pipe was. In the second place, I wouldn't get any credit. Besides, Herbst was bound to know who had sent in the letter anyway.

The sensible thing, I knew, would be to drop the whole idea. But I didn't want to; I was tired of being pushed around and called a liar. So in the end I decided I would do it. I would write a letter to the paper and sign my own name to it. It might be risky, but it was better than being pushed around.

The next day I bought some letter paper and envelopes at the drugstore, and went home and sat up in my room writing the letter. It took me a long time to get it right. I didn't want to tell any lies about it, because if they caught me lying about part of it, they wouldn't believe any of it. But I didn't want to tell the whole truth, either—about how I'd started the whole thing to get people to respect me, or about being caught by the cops, and all of that. In the end I wrote:

To the Editor:
The carpet factory is deliberately polluting the Timber River. I know because I saw a green liquid coming out of a pipe in the riverbank near the factory. This is illegal, and somebody should tell the people at Albany about it.

Yours truly,
Harry White.

I wondered if the newspaper editors knew who I was. I wondered if they knew how everybody in town looked down on us because we stole, and Helen had run off, and Dad didn't have a regular job. Would the editors decide that being as I was a White I was a liar, and they shouldn't trust what I told them? I thought about putting on some kind of a PS saying that I wasn't a liar and they could trust me, but I couldn't think of any way of saying it that wouldn't sound silly, so I let it go. And the next day, after school, I went to the post office and mailed the letter.

The *Timber Falls Journal* came out on Thursdays. I mailed my letter on Monday, which meant that I had to wait a few days before the letter came out. I was pretty excited. When the letter came out, there was bound to be a lot of talk about it around town. I wondered what the kids at school would think. They would be pretty surprised all right, and a lot of them would wish that they'd thought up the idea first.

But I was nervous, too, for there was no telling

what Herbst might do. He would want to get me if he could. The question was whether he could or not.

Finally Thursday came. It drizzled all day, and after school I walked through the drizzle to the drugstore and bought a copy of the paper. I didn't want anybody to see me reading it—I didn't know why, I just didn't. So I went across Main Street and around in front of the railroad station. There was a bench on the station platform, with a roof over it, where people used to wait when they had passenger trains. I went and sat on the bench to keep out of the drizzle, and opened the paper. My hands were shaking and I felt weak. I flipped through the paper until I came to the "Letters to the Editor" column and raced down it.

My letter wasn't there. Maybe they had decided it was so important, they would put it in another part of the paper, I thought. I went back to the first page and went through the whole newspaper from beginning to end. The letter wasn't anywhere. I started from the back and went through the whole paper again, looking as carefully as I could, just to be sure I didn't miss anything. But my letter wasn't in.

I sat there watching the drizzle fall onto the shiny steel tops of the railroad tracks, and I wondered. I didn't want to think they had decided not to run my letter because I was trash and couldn't be trusted. Maybe it took them longer than a few days to get a letter in. Maybe they had others ahead of it. Or maybe you had to get your letter in a week in advance or something. There could be a lot of reasons why my letter wasn't in the paper. There was only one thing to do, and that was wait until next week's paper. So I balled the paper up, threw it into an oil drum they had for a trash can at the station, and went on home through the drizzle.

That night, when Dad came home from work, he said less than usual. He just walked into the house, poured himself a drink of whiskey, and didn't say anything to anybody. For a while he sat there at that scratched kitchen table drinking his whiskey. Then he said, "Harry, come out to the barn. I want to talk to you."

He'd found out something, that was for sure. He went out the door, and I went out behind him in the drizzling rain. When we got out to the barn, he leaned up against the workbench, which was all cluttered with tools and rags and bits of wood. I went over and leaned against the workbench, but a little way from him, so as not to be too close. I didn't look at him but stared out into the dark drizzle at the end of the day.

"I saw your pal Herbst today," he said. "He had me come over to his office."

"Oh," I said.

"He told me the cops caught you out there by the carpet factory taking pictures."

"I wasn't doing anything wrong, Dad—"

"Shut up," he said. "I didn't say you were. He said it wasn't likely anybody would get back in there again. They're going to put a chain fence around that whole area and put a couple of dogs in there. So stay away from there from now on. You might get hurt."

"I wasn't planning on—"

"Shut up. I haven't finished." He was being mighty tough, and I didn't understand why. "Now you listen to me close, Harry." He stopped and gave me a hard look to make sure I was taking him seriously. "I want you to forget all about anything you saw in there. I don't want you to say a word about it to anybody. Hear?"

"But, Dad," I said. "They're pollut——"

He hit me. He smacked me hard across the face. It spun my head around, and I staggered away from the workbench and almost fell. I was dazed and shook my head to try to clear it. His words seemed to be coming from a distance. "I told you," he said. "Just forget about it. Just forget it for good. You hear me?"

My head was clearing. I licked my lips. I could taste salt and I knew I was bleeding. I stared at him.

"You hear me, Harry?"

I knew he would hit me again if I didn't answer. "Yes," I said in a low voice. He turned and walked out of the barn and I sat down on the rough plank floor and began to cry. My face hurt, but that wasn't it. Why was Dad siding with Herbst, after all the terrible things he'd said about Herbst? He never liked Herbst. And he'd always said he himself was against pollution.

For a long time I sat there on the barn floor. I knew that Mom and Dad were in the kitchen eating supper. I was hungry, but I didn't want to see either of them. So I went on sitting there, getting hungrier and hungrier. Finally I got up and went down to the house. Mom was washing the dishes, and Dad was in the other room watching a baseball game.

"There's some hash on the stove, Harry," Mom said in a low voice. "I kept it warm for you."

It wasn't Mom's fault that Dad had hit me, but I didn't feel like saying thank you to anybody. So I just got a plate and helped myself to some hash out of the frying pan.

"Don't be too upset with Dad," she said. "He's only doing what he thinks is right for the family."

I didn't understand that. Why was hitting me right for the family? "He didn't have to hit me," I said. I sat down at the table with my plate of hash.

She sighed. "I know," she said. "But he said you gave him an argument."

Dad came into the kitchen. I wouldn't look at him, but bent my head down and started eating. He didn't say anything but put on his jacket and went out the kitchen door. In a moment we heard the truck start and drive away. And that was when I remembered that the next Thursday my letter about the pollution would come out in the paper. I sat there frozen, a forkful of hash stopped in midair. If that letter was published, he'd give me a real beating. I didn't understand why he was so strong on me keeping my mouth shut about the pollution pipe, but he was, and he would near beat me to death when that letter came out.

ELEVEN

"What's the matter, Harry?" Mom said.

"Nothing," I said. "I just thought of something." I shoved the forkful of hash into my mouth, but I didn't feel like eating any more. If that letter was published, I'd be finished. I just had to get it back.

The next afternoon I went over to the newspaper office after school. It was just outside of town, in the downstairs of an ordinary house. There was a regular front door with a wooden sign screwed onto it saying TIMBER FALLS JOURNAL. I was feeling pretty nervous. I didn't know if I was supposed to knock, or just walk in, or what. Finally I opened the door and went in. A little fence divided the room in half. Behind the fence were a slim young man and a woman with gray hair. They sat at desks heaped with papers, and beside each desk was a typewriter on a little green metal table. Behind them an open door led to another room. I could see a part of a desk through the open door.

The woman looked up at me. "Yes?" she said.

"I sent a letter to the editor last week," I said. "I changed my mind about getting it printed. I'd like to get it back if it isn't too late," I said, trying to be polite.

She smiled. "You changed your mind?"

"I decided I didn't want to get it printed," I said.

"We don't always print the letters we get," she said. "We might not have planned to print yours."

That was a relief, but I had to be sure. "It was about pollution at the carpet factory."

She gave me a funny look. "Oh, that letter," she said.

"Yes," I said. "I hope you won't print it."

She got up and walked through the open door into the room behind her. In a minute she came back and sat down at her desk again. An older man appeared at the open door. He had a gray mustache and was wearing an unbuttoned vest. He was smoking a pipe. For a minute he stood in the doorway looking at me. It made me feel like I'd done something wrong. "You wrote that letter?" he said finally.

"Yes," I said. I figured he was the editor. "I hope I can get it back, if it isn't a lot of trouble," I said, still trying to be polite.

He sort of nibbled on the mouthpiece of the pipe. "You're one of the Whites from Mountain Pass Road?"

I hated that. "Yes," I said.

But at least he didn't tell me to go away. "Come on in for a minute."

I opened the gate in the fence, went between the

two desks and into the back room. He had a big desk, which was also covered with papers, and a type-writer on a green metal table. There was a faded rug on the floor, bookshelves filled with books on one wall, a huge map of the Adirondacks on another, and a big, worn overstuffed chair in one corner. He pointed to the armchair. "Have a seat." I sat down, and he went behind the desk and sat down.

He nibbled at the pipe a little and then took a puff on it. "You actually saw a pipe out there by the carpet factory? Actually spilling something into the river?"

For a minute I thought about telling him it was all a lie, that I'd made the whole thing up. But I didn't want to make my reputation any worse than I had to. "Yes, I saw it. But I want to forget about it."

"Tell me exactly what you saw," he said.

That worried me. It sounded like he was trying to get information for a story. "I'd just as soon—"

"Don't worry," he said. "I'm not going to get you in trouble. Just tell me what it was."

There wasn't much of a way around it. "Well, it looked like a twelve-inch iron pipe sticking out of the bank and angling down toward the water. It's pretty hard to spot because there's a lot of foliage around it, and if you weren't looking for it, you probably wouldn't notice. But there's a furrow below the pipe running down to the water. You can tell there's been chemicals coming out of the pipe, because nothing is growing there."

"So you didn't actually see anything come out of it?"

"Yes, I did," I said. "I went up there one night with

a flashlight, and I saw chemicals or something coming out." I decided not to mention the pictures I'd taken.

He squinted at me and took another puff on the pipe. "You actually saw something pouring into the river."

"Yes."

"What did it look like?"

"Like greenish water," I said.

"You're positive."

"Yes." He didn't say anything for a minute. Then he said, "What were you doing out there?"

I was afraid he would ask that. I didn't want to tell the truth. I didn't want to say anything about not wanting to be trash anymore. I didn't want to talk to him about being trash at all. So I told my old story. "I was looking for birds. Somebody said they saw a pileated woodpecker up there. They're rare."

He nodded. "Yes, I know they're rare. A couple of times we've done stories when somebody's spotted one." I could tell that he believed my story. "Why did you go back at night?"

Suddenly I began to wonder how much he knew about what I'd been doing. Had the cops told him that they'd picked me up out there with a flash camera? Maybe they had. I decided I'd better stick as close to the truth as I could. "I saw that pipe the first time I was out there, and I figured that was where the pollution was coming from. I figured that if they were dumping stuff, they would do it at night. I just went back to see if they were."

"That's when you saw liquid running from the pipe?"

"Yes, but then somebody spotted me from the factory and called the cops. They said I was trespassing and took me down to the station house."

"I'll bet they did," he said. His pipe had gone out, and he lit it with a lighter. "Did they charge you with anything?"

I decided it was best to keep Mr. Herbst and all that out of it. "No, they just let me go and told me not to hang around there anymore. But please," I said. "I don't want anybody to know about it now."

He puffed on his pipe, blowing smoke around the place. "I'm curious," he said. "How come you changed your mind?"

I couldn't think of anything to say. I hadn't figured anybody was going to ask me a lot of questions, and I hadn't worked out a story. I felt myself go red, and then I looked down at my hands. Finally I said, "I don't want to discuss it. I just changed my mind."

"Cops say anything about keeping your mouth shut?"

I shook my head. "They just said to stay away from there."

"Somebody offer you some money to withdraw the letter?"

When he said that, something came to me: Had Herbst bribed Dad to keep me quiet? Would he have done something like that? Would Dad have taken a bribe from somebody he hated? When I thought about it, I knew he would. He'd say that if they were stupid enough to offer him some money, he'd be glad to take it. "No," I said. "Nobody offered me any money."

"You sure?"

"I'm positive. I wouldn't take a bribe."

He knocked his pipe out on a big ashtray on his desk. "And you won't tell me why you changed your mind about it."

I couldn't tell him the real reason. He'd want to know why Dad had hit me, why Dad was so serious about keeping the whole thing quiet. I knew there wouldn't be very good answers to that. I wondered: If Dad *had* taken a bribe, could they send him to jail for that? To be honest, I wouldn't have minded him going to jail, but who would pay the rent? I said, "Nobody offered me any money. I just don't want to discuss it."

He started to fill his pipe again from a leather pouch. "Well," he said. "You don't have to worry about it. There was no way we were going to run that letter. As a matter of fact, I burned it."

What a relief that was. I was safe from Dad. But I was pretty surprised too. "You burned my letter?"

"Harry— You said your name is Harry?"

"Yes."

"Harry, you're not the only person in town who knows what's going on up there. I've known for years that they've been polluting the Timber River. Some of the guys who work up there know. The union shop steward knows, because I've talked to him about it. Some of the town officials know, because I've talked to them too. And the fishermen all know because you can't eat the trout out of there anymore. It's got a taste to it."

Well, that was about the biggest surprise I'd ever had. I just sat there with my mouth open, feeling sort of silly. "If they all know, why hasn't anybody done something about it?"

"It's simple. Fred Herbst has said the main office will close down the factory if they force him to put in pollution controls. The carpet factory is just part of a larger company. They say that the factory isn't profitable as it is, that they're only keeping it open for the good of the town, and so forth."

"Is that true?" I said. "Isn't it profitable?"

He shrugged. "You'll never know and I'll never know. There's no way the town can force them to open their books, and even if we did, they probably have the accounting worked out to make it look unprofitable whether it is or not."

"Is it legal to do that?"

"Sure, if the tax people accept it. But it doesn't really matter. Herbst says that if the factory is forced to put in pollution controls, they'll have to close, and people around here aren't willing to take the chance. This area has been depressed for a long, long time. That carpet factory provides a lot of jobs to people around here, and those people cash their checks in the local stores. You walk into one of the supermarkets some Friday night when they're in there with their families, and watch those cash registers ringing up eighty, ninety, a hundred dollars at a clip. Close the carpet factory and you'd close half the stores in town."

"Doesn't anyone care about the river being polluted?"

The editor puffed out a mouthful of smoke. "Sure they do," he said. "Given their choice, people would rather see the Timber River cleaned up. But to most people being out of work is an awful lot worse than a little pollution."

There was something about it I didn't understand. "You mean that people like the town officials and the union shop steward and whoever knew about it got together and decided to keep quiet about it?"

He frowned, puffed on his pipe, and thought for a minute. "Well, not exactly. I don't doubt that the town councilmen have discussed the whole thing quietly among themselves. I know for a fact that about five years back the Sportsmen's Club invited Herbst to their monthly meeting. That's a matter of record. I covered the meeting for the paper. That's when Herbst made it clear that the factory would be closed if they were forced to put in pollution controls. I front-paged the story. After that people just decided to shut up about it. It wasn't a question of getting together on it. They just quietly shut up."

I just sat there. I didn't know what to say. My whole idea had been wrong from the beginning. It had all been a waste of effort. I felt plain stupid. "So it wouldn't have mattered even if I'd brought you in pictures of the pollution or something."

He shook his head. "I'm not going to run that story. Not until there's popular support for it." He puffed and then gazed at the smoke slowly curling and twisting upward. "I was considering it. At the time that Herbst told the Sportsmen's Club that he'd close the factory if they tried to do anything about pollution controls, I considered really going to town on it. I'd just got started checking into it when I got a phone call from the president of the Merchants' Association. He told me flat out that if I started a crusade against the factory, all the stores in town would pull their advertising out of the paper. I figure Herbst had leaned on him, but he wouldn't admit it. You can't run a newspaper without advertising—no advertising, no paper."

"You mean the store owners can tell you what stories to run?"

"Harry, no newspaper can afford to offend its advertisers. You can do it occasionally, up to a point. But you can't do it very often. And you certainly can't take a stand directly opposite to what they think are their best interests. That's just the way it is."

"Isn't polluting against the law? Aren't the councilmen supposed to stop it if they know somebody's doing it?"

He thought about that for a minute. "Of course, there are state and federal laws of various kinds, pretty strict ones too. But it wouldn't be up to the councilmen to do anything unless there were antipollution laws on the town books. It wouldn't be their jurisdiction." He thought some more. "I don't know whether Timber Falls has an antipollution ordinance or not."

"But if it did, the councilmen would have to enforce it, right?"

He thought about it. Then he said, "Harry, if you

want to make a crusade of this, that's up to you. But I'm warning you, if you do, your dad will never get another day's work in Timber Falls, and nobody around here will ever speak to you again. I'm serious. And it might be a lot worse than that. A fellow who thinks he'll be out of work, and likely to lose a home that he's spent twenty years working for, will do almost anything to stop it."

TWELVE

Three days later Dad drove into the yard at supper time with a brand-new Ford ton-and-a-half truck. Mom saw it through the window and said, "Here comes Dad with the new truck."

"New truck?" I said. "Dad bought a new truck?"

"He worked out a deal with the man."

We ran out into the backyard. Dad was standing next to it with his hand on the door panel, kind of patting it. It was a beauty—maroon, and it had a winch on the front. Everything on it shone like jewels. Dad just stood next to it patting it and grinning. I couldn't remember when I'd seen him smile that much. "How do you like it?" he said.

"It's a beauty, Dad," I said.

"Look inside, Harry," he said, smiling some more. "It's got everything—AM and FM, CB, the works." I looked inside. It had that new-car smell, the seats were shiny and clean, and there wasn't a speck of dust on anything. It was something all right. "Now, I want you to keep it clean, Harry," he said. "That's your job. And if you do it right, I'll teach you how to drive it."

It was the binoculars all over again—beautiful as could be but with a kind of rotten odor to it, so that I was drawn to it and driven away from it at the same time. For, of course, he'd bought it with his bribe money from Herbst. I didn't know whether Herbst had given him enough money to buy the whole thing. Probably not; probably he'd given him part of it, and Dad would pay the rest on time. It didn't matter. To get that beautiful new truck he'd ruined my plan for getting something done about the pollution in the Timber River. He'd sold me out. And I resolved right then and there that I wasn't going to keep the truck clean. I wasn't going to lay a finger on it. He could do it himself.

Of course, he wanted to take us for a drive. I didn't want to go, but there wasn't any way I could say no. We got in. There was plenty of room for the three of us in the cab. "It's a lot better than the old truck, Harry," Dad said. "You won't have to ride in the back when we go someplace." He'd already forgotten about Helen. Then he began telling me about clutching and shifting and the rest of that. I knew a lot about that already anyway.

I thought about it later when I was sitting on the back steps watching the stars wink on one by one. I didn't want to be any part of the truck, or Dad, or anything. I didn't want to learn to drive on it, and I didn't want Dad to teach me to drive. I didn't want him to do anything for me. Not that he'd ever done very much. He'd taken me up into the mountains a couple of times and stolen me a pair of binoculars. But now I didn't want him to do anything for me at all. If he was to offer me a hundred bucks out of his bribe money, I wouldn't take it. I didn't want any part of it.

What made me the maddest about it was his interfering in the whole carpet factory thing. It wasn't any of his business. He had no right to do it. He had no right to interfere. Sitting there on the back steps, I stopped watching the stars come out, and began to get mad. I wished there was something I could do about it. So what if everybody in Timber Falls was sore at me. Nobody there liked me anyway. So what if Dad wouldn't be able to get any more jobs around there. Why did I care about that? It could all go to pieces as far as I was concerned. I'd just as soon see everything go to pieces anyway.

I wondered if there was anything I could do about it. I wondered if there was any way to get the town councilmen to do something. The newspaper editor had said that if there was some law on the books of the town, they might have to do something. At least that's what I thought he said. I sat there trying to remember. It seemed right to me. If there was a law, they'd have to do something about it.

Suppose there was a law—would I really be able to do anything about it? Would I really *want* to do anything about it? If I made a lot of trouble over it, would everybody in town stop giving Dad work? They might, I figured. What would happen then? Dad would give me a real beating, that was for sure. What else? I didn't know.

But at least I could find out about it. I could find out whether there were any laws on the books about polluting. So the next day after school I went to the old redbrick town hall, with a pen and my assignment notebook. The town hall had been built in 1890 when there had been a lot of logging in the area and the town was richer. You could tell when it had been built, because the date was carved into a slab of stone over the door. I hadn't been in the town hall very often. I'd gone in there that time our social studies class had studied the town, and I'd been there a couple of times when Dad had business there. I couldn't remember what. The place had a musty smell. The floors had got dirt ground into them that you'd never get out, and the radiators were old and banged and whistled.

I went in and stood in the hall looking around. I saw doors with little signs above them which stuck out into the hall: ASSESSOR, ZONING COMMISSION, TOWN COUNCILMEN. Finally I saw the town clerk's office. The door was open and I went in. There wasn't much to it: just a room with a couple of women sitting behind desks, a table with a few books lying on it, some filing cabinets, a picture of George Washington and a big map of the town hanging on the wall. One of the women was young and had blond hair. The other was older and fat; she had a big dish of candy on her desk. "Yes?" the blond one said.

"I'm doing a school project," I said. "I have to find out what laws the town has on pollution."

"Pollution?"

"Air pollution and so forth," I said, to throw them off.

"Pollution," the fat woman said. "Are they going to start up again?" She took a candy out of the bowl and unwrapped it. "Want one, Jeanette?" she said to the blonde.

"I better start watching my weight," the blonde said. "I won't be able to get into my new dress." She looked back at me. "What do you want to know, exactly?"

"The pollution laws," I said. "What the pollution laws are."

"It's a school report?" she said.

The fat woman put the candy into her mouth. "Some of these teachers ought to learn to keep their noses out of things."

"Who's your teacher?" the blond woman said.

I was getting myself into trouble, because if they checked up they'd find out I was lying. I began to feel a little sweaty. "Mrs. Heinz."

"It isn't a very popular subject in Timber Falls," the younger woman said.

"Well, I don't know about that," I said. "I just have to find out if the town has any laws about it."

The blond woman sighed, got up, and went over to one of the filing cabinets. She opened a drawer and took out a big loose-leaf notebook filled with photocopies. "Here's the town code," she said. "Be careful with it. Sit over at that table and see if you can find what you want."

So I did. The town code was pretty confusing.

There was a table of contents in the front, but it didn't say anything about pollution or the environment. I tried a couple of other topics that seemed like they might be right, like water, rivers, and air; but they weren't. Finally I just gave up and began going through it one page at a time, scanning each page in hopes of hitting what I was looking for. It was pretty boring, and when I'd spent an hour and had only got a quarter of the way through the loose-leaf pages, I got discouraged and was ready to give up.

But I made myself keep going by telling myself that if I didn't find anything in another half an hour, I could quit, and about fifteen minutes later I found something. It said: "Town Ordinance #3762 Enacted February 17, 1969, in Respect to the Quality of the Environment." The ordinance was about a page long, and I read it all the way through. It was pretty hard for me to understand. Some of it I couldn't figure out at all—I just didn't know what some of the words meant. But the basic idea was clear enough: Nobody was supposed to dump *anything* in any of the rivers or creeks around town. You weren't supposed to throw in even a cigarette butt or pieces of bread for the geese when they came through in spring and fall. You could fish, you could swim, and you could have a boat on the rivers, although most of them were too small or had too many rapids for boats. But you couldn't dump anything in.

So the laws were there all right. And the next question in my mind was whether the town councilmen *had* to enforce the laws. Could they ignore laws if they chose? That was the next thing I had to find out.

I copied out of the town code book the parts about throwing stuff in the rivers, then I gave the book back to the blond woman. "Did you find what you were looking for?" she said.

"I think so," I said.

"People ought to watch where they put their noses," the fat woman said.

I blushed a little, and went outside to think about it. Who would know if the town councilmen had to enforce the pollution laws? The newspaper editor would know. I figured he was probably busy and wouldn't want to be bothered by me, but it was worth trying anyway. So I went down Main Street and out the side road to the newspaper office. When I walked in, the editor was standing in the front room. His pipe was in his mouth, and he was putting on his jacket. "You're back again," he said.

"Yes, sir," I said, to be polite. "I wanted to ask you something."

He frowned and looked at his wristwatch. "I've only got a minute," he said.

"It won't take long," I said.

He nodded toward the open door to his back office. "Okay, come on in."

I followed him in. He sat down at his desk with his jacket on, and I stood in front of the desk. "I looked up the town code," I said.

"Oh?" he said.

"There's a law all right," I said. I showed him what I'd written in my notebook.

He took the notebook, read it over, and handed it

back to me. "So you're going to do something about it after all?"

"I don't know," I said. "I'm thinking about it."

"I'll say this," he said. "You've got a lot of guts."

When he said that, the funniest feeling swept over me. I didn't understand it. I felt sort of warm and dazed. For a minute I forgot what I was going to say, what I was doing there, why I had come. I stood there feeling that feeling.

"So what did you want to ask me?" he said.

I remembered where I was. "Well, the thing is, do the town councilmen have to enforce the law, or can they decide which laws they want to enforce?"

"Oh, no, they have to enforce the laws," he said.

"Why haven't they, then?"

"Well, for one thing, that law was passed a long time ago. They probably don't even know it's on the books. But more important, they know the people of this town would run them out of office if they tried to enforce it." He took the pipe out of his mouth and pointed it at me. "Harry, I admire your attitude," he said. Once again that funny feeling rolled over me. "But you're going to get yourself into an awful lot of trouble if you go on with this. And you're not going to do the town any good."

"Maybe Herbst is just bluffing," I said. "Maybe he won't really close the factory if they have to put in pollution controls."

He stood up. "You might be right," he said. "But nobody around here wants to take the chance." He looked at his watch again. "I've got to go," he said, and gestured toward the door. I went out, and he came along behind me. When we were outside on the street, he stopped and put his hand on my shoulder. "I didn't want to say this inside in front of the others. Do you realize that Herbst gave your Dad five thousand dollars to make you keep quiet?"

Five thousand. The truck probably cost around fifteen thousand. I was surprised he knew about it. "I know," I said. "Dad bought a new truck."

"Your dad wanted Herbst to give him a truck. They settled on five thousand dollars. What's he going to say when he finds out you're not shutting up?"

He certainly knew a lot about everything. It was beginning to sound like a bunch of them were getting together on it. "He'd give me an awful beating if he found out," I said.

He looked at me. "Don't you think that's a pretty good reason to drop it? Your dad has his faults, but he's always kept a roof over your head and food on your plate. He won't be able to do that anymore if you go on with this."

I knew I shouldn't ask, but I couldn't help myself: "How come you know so much about it?"

"Harry, I've been editing this paper for over twenty years. I know things about Timber Falls you wouldn't believe. That's the business I'm in. After you'd been into the office the last time, I called Herbst. I wanted to find out what he was doing. I wanted to know what was going on just in case there was a story in it after all. I don't want to be scooped by some other newspaper in my own town. I try to keep on top of things. That's my job after all." He looked at his watch again. "I really have to go. I'll just say once again, you don't know what kind of mess this could blow up into. I think you ought to drop it."

I looked at him. "I don't know," I said.

He shook his head. "You're a gutsy kid all right." Then he turned and walked away, and I stood there with that feeling running over me again. It was a feeling I'd never had before. Then suddenly I got what it was: It was the first time in my whole life that I remembered anybody saying anything nice to me, outside of the family. I'd never had anybody admire me before.

I started to walk on home feeling kind of funny and surprised. My thoughts flashed here and there without much sense to them. The funny thing was, with the editor saying all those good things about me—that I was gutsy and he admired my attitude and all that—I wasn't so sore about the whole thing anymore. Maybe I was doing wrong to keep on with it. Maybe it wasn't right; maybe it was the wrong thing to do. Maybe I ought to just drop the whole thing.

Suddenly I realized that it was getting on toward supper time. I started to walk faster. But just then Dad came along in the new truck and picked me up. My good mood went away. I just didn't like being with him.

He was monitoring the CB. Some guy was talking about an accident over on the state highway. "Harry, I took the truck up the old tote road this afternoon. It just waltzed up that steep hill in third, just waltzed up it. Maybe over the weekend I'll start teaching you how to drive it."

He was pretty cheerful about that truck all right,

but I didn't want to talk about it. I didn't want to talk about anything to him. So I sat there quiet.

"Cat got your tongue?"

"No," I said. "I'm just tired is all."

"You getting enough sleep?"

"Sure," I said. "I'm just tired." Luckily we got to the house just then, and I could stop talking to him. We pulled into the driveway, and we hadn't even gotten out of the truck when Mom came running out of the house. It startled me because Mom didn't usually come running anyplace like that. "Frank," she cried. "Frank. The police called. They arrested Helen."

We jumped out of the truck. "Arrested?" Dad said. "Where is she?"

"In New York. They found her in New York. She's in jail. My poor baby." She began to cry.

"Stop wailing, Doris," Dad said. "What did they get her for?"

Tears were running down Mom's cheeks. "Drugs," she said. "They say she was selling drugs. And prostitution."

THIRTEEN

Dad got back into the truck and drove into town to talk to the police, and I sat there with Mom, saying things like maybe it wasn't true, maybe they'd got her mixed up with somebody else. It didn't make her feel any better. Of course, I knew it was all true. But I couldn't say that to Mom.

Finally Dad got back with the story. Helen had got picked up for prostitution, along with the women she was living with. When they searched her purse, they found a lot of cocaine in it. At first she wouldn't tell them where she came from or anything, but then they said they would send her away for a couple of years, so she told them who she was. She was over sixteen and they could charge her, but they were willing to send her home in the custody of her parents if she'd go. The New York cops called our cops, and they worked it out so that Dad could drive down to New York and get her. So he fixed himself a thermos of coffee and set off to drive to New York. It would take him maybe six hours to get there and six hours to get back.

It was terrible. Now it was going to go all over town that Helen was a prostitute. Nobody in Timber Falls would ever talk to her again. Not even Charlie Fritz. And nobody would talk to me either. As far as us ever getting over being trash around there, that was finished. I could become a general in the air force and I'd still be trash so far as Timber Falls was concerned. Before we'd been no-good; now we would be nothing at all. I wondered if the storekeepers would even let us in their stores anymore. I wondered if they would serve us.

The funny thing was, I didn't feel sore at Helen. I just felt so sorry for her. It was going to be terrible for her to ride for six hours in the truck with Dad. He'd hit her. He was bound to do that. He wouldn't feel sorry for her at all. He'd bawl her out the whole way and belt her if she answered him back. But that wouldn't be the worst of it. The terrible part would be going to school and having all the kids stare at her and talk about her. Nobody would want to eat with her at lunch. They would get up and move if she sat down near them. I didn't know how she would be able to stand that. I felt so sorry for her.

That night, sitting on the back steps, I thought about it. And what it seemed to me was this: Here was poor Helen who'd never done anything wrong to anybody, who only wanted to get some boy to like her; and who had had to wash her own clothes since she was eight years old; and who had never got much of anything from anybody; here she was, a disgrace and an outcast. And Herbst who was polluting the Timber River, lying about it, and bribing people was rich and respected and could do anything he wanted. And the newspaper editor who had known all about the pollution for years and was covering up for it was respected and admired around Timber Falls. And the merchants around town who had pressured the newspaper editor to shut up about it—they were making good money and were respected in the town. And all the other people in Timber Falls who knew about it and had kept their mouths shut. And Dad who had taken a bribe to force me to shut up was going to belt Helen good for what she had done. Was it right? Was it fair? Maybe the stars would never begin to fall.

Suddenly I didn't care what people thought of me anymore. I didn't give a damn, not a single damn. I grit my teeth. I knew what I was going to do: I was going to get revenge on all of them for Helen. I was going to make the biggest stink about the pollution that I could, and close the carpet factory down.

What was the best way to do it? I wasn't sure. I could start with the town council. They were supposed to be enforcing the law, weren't they? I couldn't remember exactly what the town ordinance said, so I got up and went inside to look for the assignment notebook I'd written it down in.

The notebook wasn't anywhere in the kitchen or the living room. I didn't remember going up to my room since I'd been home. I'd been too busy trying to cheer Mom up. But I went upstairs and looked anyway. It wasn't in my room. There wasn't that much stuff in my room that you could lose anything there.

So I went back downstairs and looked in the kitchen again, and all of a sudden I realized where it was. I stood still, frozen, in the middle of the kitchen, my hand in midair like I was catching something. I'd left the notebook in the truck. It had been lying on the seat beside me, and when Mom had come running out of the house shouting that Helen was in jail, I'd forgotten all about the notebook and just jumped out of the truck. It must still be there, lying on the seat, opened to the page with the pollution ordinance written on it. Dad would just have to take one look, and after that he'd kill me.

But maybe it had fallen out of the truck when I'd jumped out. Sometimes that happened. I got a flashlight and went out to the dirt driveway and looked all around where the truck had been when I'd jumped out. It wasn't there.

There was still a chance that Dad wouldn't notice it lying on the seat, especially if his mind was on Helen and all. Or that it fell off the seat onto the floor where he wouldn't notice it. Or that it slid into the crack between the seat and the door and would fall onto the street when Helen opened the passenger door to get in. All I could do was hope.

But losing the notebook wasn't going to stop me from getting revenge for Helen. I don't know why I thought of it that way—as getting revenge. She didn't have anything to do with it really. She wasn't much interested in whether anyone was polluting the Timber River. But still, it seemed like revenge to me. And I was bound and determined to do it.

Was there any way I could do it without Dad finding out? There might be. I wouldn't go to a town council meeting. I'd just go to see one of the councilmen privately and hear what he had to say. After that I'd figure out what to do next.

So I had decided that. I turned off the flashlight and went back to the house. Mom was sitting in the living room watching TV. I figured she was planning on staying up until Helen got home. I figured she would have trouble going to sleep anyway until they were back. But I didn't see how they would get home until morning, so I went to bed.

When I got up in the morning, the TV was still going and Mom was asleep in her chair in front of it. I quietly shut it off, fixed myself some peanut butter on toast for breakfast, and went to school. I wasn't looking forward to it very much because of everybody knowing what had happened to Helen. But nobody said anything, and I figured word hadn't got around yet. And after school I went back to the old redbrick town hall and went inside.

For a minute I stood there smelling the musty smell and listening to the radiators bang. A couple of doors down the hall I could see a sign saying TOWN COUNCIL. I went down there and listened by the door. No noise came from inside. I took a deep breath and opened the door. The room was empty except for a couple of desks, some wooden chairs against a wall, some filing cabinets, and an American flag.

I shut the door again and went back to the town

clerk's office. The same two women were sitting there. The fat one was unwrapping a candy from her bowl. "I'm being naughty today," she said. "I've already eaten four of these." Then she saw me. "You're back? What is it this time?"

"Nothing," I said. "I was just wondering if any of the town councilmen were around."

"What's this about?" she said. She looked suspicious.

"Mr. Novick might be in around four," the blond one said. I had a half hour to wait. So I went outside and sat on the steps. I leaned up against the redbrick wall and worked on my English homework. After a while a Volkswagen Rabbit pulled up, and a youngish man wearing chinos and a blue flannel shirt got out. He came up the steps and passed me to go into the town hall. I figured it might be Mr. Novick, so I followed him in. He stopped at the town clerk's office and asked for his mail. The blond woman handed him some letters. "This kid wants to talk to you," she said.

He looked around at me. "Sure, what is it, son?" He seemed like a pretty cheerful guy.

"It's sort of private," I said.

He smiled. "Okay, let's go down to the office." Smiling like that, he was making me feel hopeful. He went down to the town council's office, and I followed him in. He sat down behind one of the desks, and I stood there until he told me to sit down in one of the wooden chairs. He looked through his mail for a couple of minutes, frowning and dropping the envelopes onto the desk, and then he looked up at me and smiled again and said, "Okay, what is it?"

I took a deep breath and said, "I've got proof that the carpet factory is polluting the Timber River."

His smile went away like something you wipe off a blackboard. He looked at me and then he said, "What's your name?"

Here it came again. "Harry White."

"From Mountain Pass Road."

"Yes," I said.

He put his hands together in front of his face like he was praying into them, and sat there thinking and looking out over his hands at me. All the while I kept getting more and more nervous until I wanted to jump out of the chair. Finally he took his hands away from his face and said, "I figured that's who you were. I've been hearing about you."

I wondered who he had heard it from. Herbst? The newspaper editor? The cops? Who else was in on it? I figured it was most likely the cops who had told him. "I saw it myself," I said.

"Look, Harry, I think you ought to forget all about this."

"It's against the law," I said.

"That's no news," he said. "We all know that. But that isn't the point." He looked at me some more. Then he said, "I thought your dad told you to drop it."

He knew about that too. He couldn't have got that from the cops. He must have got it from the newspaper editor or Herbst. "He did. He belted me good and told me to forget about it. I decided not to."

"Harry, what got you into this thing in the first place?"

"I did it on my own," I said. I was tired of lying about it, and I decided to tell the truth, all except the part about being trash. I would never discuss that with anybody. "I knew they were dumping stuff in the river, because when I went out to the river to watch the fish, I could see it. I decided to investigate, so I went out there and found that pipe." I figured if he knew as much about it as he did, he'd know about the pipe too.

He drummed his fingers on the desktop. "Are you telling me that nobody put you up to this—some environmental group or something?"

I shook my head. "Nobody did," I said. "I figured it out for myself."

"And you saw the pipe. But you didn't actually see anything coming out of it, did you?"

"Yes, I did. I went out there with a flashlight one night and I saw it."

"How do you know it was chemicals? Maybe it was ordinary waste water."

"It wasn't," I said. "It was greenish. Besides, nothing was growing underneath the pipe."

"Okay," he said. "Let's say I believe that you did this yourself. And let's say I believe that you really saw the stuff. If you make an issue out of it, you're going to stir up a lot of trouble around town. There are a lot of angles to it you don't understand. This is something for us adults to worry about. You worry about your schoolwork, and let us worry about this."

"Maybe they really wouldn't close the carpet factory," I said. "Maybe they're just bluffing."

He gave me a funny look. "You know about that, huh?"

"Yes," I said.

"Well, then maybe you can understand that around here jobs matter a lot more than a little bit of pollution."

"It isn't a little bit," I said. I was beginning to get stubborn, and I knew I was going to lose my temper soon.

"Okay, a lot. It still doesn't matter stacked up against people's jobs."

"But maybe they're bluffing," I said. "Why can't you—"

He slammed his hand down on the desk. "You're meddling in something you don't know anything about. You're going to end up causing a lot of trouble for the people in this town. Stop giving me that baloney that you're doing this on your own. Who put you up to it?"

He was angry, and I was scared, but I wasn't going to give in. "Nobody put me up to it. Don't call me a liar."

He slammed his hand on the desk again. "I'll call you whatever I want to call you, son. You're just out to make trouble because that's the kind you are. You and your whole family."

I jumped up. "You can't say that to me," I shouted.

He jumped up, too, and his chair crashed over behind him. "Oh, yes, I can," he shouted. "If you go any further with this, we're going to run you and your lousy family out of Timber Falls. You're nothing but trash anyway, lying and stealing and now your sister—"

I grabbed up the chair behind me and swung it over my head. "You say anything more about my sister and I'll kill you," I shouted.

He jumped around the desk. I started to swing it around, but he was a lot bigger than me, and he grabbed it before I could get in a good swing. He started to jerk it away from me. I let go and turned and ran out of the office, and down the corridor and out of the building. Once I was outside, I looked back. He was standing at the door of the town hall, but he wasn't coming after me. I turned and walked on toward home, so mad and hurt I couldn't stop crying. The tears kept running down my face until I was almost home.

FOURTEEN

Helen was sitting in the living room next to Mom, watching a soap opera. "Hi, Helen," I said. I was glad to see her. I was feeling pretty awful about everything, and I was glad to have somebody I could tell it to.

She gave me a scared look.

"I'm not sore at you," I said. "I figured it wasn't your fault."

She looked relieved and got up and gave me a hug.

"My poor baby," Mom said.

"Let's go out back," I said. So we went outside and sat on the back steps. "I'm glad you came back," I said. "I didn't have anybody to talk to."

She got a tough look on her face. "I'm going to run away again as soon as I can. I've got six months probation, after that I can leave. I'll be seventeen anyway."

"Are you supposed to go to school?"

"Yes, but I'm not going to," she said. "I'm not going to have all those dumb kids staring at me all day long.

I'm not going anyplace where I have to see Charlie Fritz. I'm going to get a job over in Watertown. As a waitress in a luncheonette. Dad says he can fix it up. Dad says he'll take me to the Watertown bus every morning."

I didn't say anything. I knew I shouldn't ask whether she was really a prostitute, but I was pretty curious. "What was it like, Helen?"—which was a way of asking so she didn't have to answer.

"It wasn't so bad," she said. "I didn't mind it so much."

"You didn't?" I said.

Then she bent over, covered her face with her hands, and began to cry. "I hated it," she said. "It was awful. But the other girls teased me for being proud." She started sobbing so hard, she couldn't speak for a minute, and I put my arm around her shoulder. Her sobbing eased up a little. "Then I found out that if I got high and drank some wine, it wasn't so bad. That's why I got all that coke. I was going to try to make money that way." She stopped sobbing, wiped her eyes on her shirt, and sat there looking calm. "It was a dumb idea. If they'd caught me just for prostitution, it wouldn't have been such a big deal. They wouldn't have called up Dad."

"Well," I said. "I'm glad you're back."

"I was homesick," she said. "I didn't think I would be. How could anyone be homesick for this dump?"

"Mom missed you," I said. "She kept saying 'My poor baby' and stuff like that. She cried sometimes."

Helen frowned. "I don't care," she said. "I'm going to leave again as soon as I can."

"Even if it makes you homesick?"

"You get over being homesick," she said. "The other women told me that. They said they were homesick, too, when they first came to New York, but they got over it in a few weeks."

"Are you going back to New York?"

"No," she said. "Not there. Someplace else. Someplace where nobody knows me and I can start over again from the beginning. Where nobody knows about our family and going to school dirty and Dad stealing, and—" Suddenly she stopped and looked at me. "I didn't mean to say that," she said.

"I already knew he stole," I said. "I didn't know you knew."

"I found out years ago," she said. "I didn't want you to know."

That surprised me. "How did you find out?"

"Remember that bike I had, the first one?" she said.

"The one you gave me?"

"Yes," she said. "I knew the kid he stole it from. That's why I had to paint it—so nobody would recognize it."

"You knew it was stolen all along?"

"Yes," she said. "But I couldn't give it back. Dad would have thought I lost it."

"He hit me—" I began, but then we heard the sound of the truck, and in a moment it came up the driveway. I stood up, feeling scared and nervous, not knowing what to expect. The truck pulled to a stop. For a moment Dad sat in the cab looking over to where we were sitting on the back steps. Then he got out of the truck. He was carrying my assignment notebook. He came slowly across the backyard toward me. When he got up to me, he said, "Come to the barn," in a quiet voice.

"No," I said.

"What?" he said. He came up so close to me that I could hear him breathing. "I said come up to the barn."

"I'm not going to," I said.

He stared at me, his face close to mine. "I thought I told you to forget about that carpet factory business."

"I'm not going to do what you say anymore," I said. "You're a thief and a liar. You're nothing but—"

He grabbed me by my shirtfront. I tried to twist away, but his grip was too tight. He slammed me across the face with his open hand. My head rang, and I heard Helen shriek. I felt dizzy, and I swung out, not knowing what I was aiming for, and caught him in the gut. He grunted and slammed me across the face again. I shook my head, trying to clear it, and swung at him again. This time I caught him in the chest. He swung back his arm. Helen shrieked again. Then she jumped on his back and began clawing his face with her fingernails. He gave me a sort of push, and I staggered backward, but I didn't fall. He reached around behind him, grabbed hold of Helen by the arm, and jerked her loose from him. She fell down. I started toward him, but he didn't move. Long red lines down his face were oozing blood. His mouth was twisted, and he was breathing hard. I stood there waiting to see what he would do. If he went for Helen, I was going to tackle him. I figured if I got him down, the two of us could do a pretty good job on him.

He touched his cheek and looked at his fingers to see the blood. "Get out of here," he said. "The two of you pack and git. Now."

Mom came out onto the back steps. "My God," she said. "Oh, my God." She put her hands over her face. "What have you done to them, Frank?"

"You shut up," he said. Then he went in the house.

I stood there feeling dizzy. My head hurt, and my nose and mouth were bleeding. "Someday I'm going to kill him," I said. "Someday."

Mom came down the steps and took me by the arm. "Are you all right, Harry? What did he do to you?"

"I'm going to kill him," I said. I spit out blood.

"Don't say things like that," Mom said.

"I got him good," Helen said. "Next time I'll use a knife."

"Helen, don't say things like that," Mom cried.

We heard water running in the kitchen sink, and I knew Dad was washing his face where Helen had scratched him. Then he came out of the house. For a minute he stood there looking at us. Then he said, "I told the two of you to git. I don't want to find you here when I get back." Then he walked past us, got into the truck, and drove away.

"Don't pay any attention to him," Mom said. "He'll get over it. He's just mad. He'll get over it."

She was right, I figured. If I stayed clear of him for

a couple of days, and let him see that I wasn't doing anything more about the carpet factory, he'd get over it. But I knew *I* wouldn't get over it. I would never get over it. And I was going to get out of there as soon as I could—in a few days, a week, a month. As soon as I could work something out I was going to leave. I had an idea about where I might go too. I figured my grandpa and grandma might want to have me. They might let me live with them until I graduated. Maybe they would want to have Helen too. I would see.

And there was another thing. I was never going to worry about being trash again. That was for sure. I'd learned something. I hadn't been able to do anything about the carpet factory polluting the Timber River, and I saw now that I would never be able to do anything about it. Even if I got somebody from Albany to come up, they wouldn't find anything. The whole town would cover it up. The town council and the newspaper editor and Herbst and everybody would cover it up, and anyway, who was going to believe one fourteen-year-old kid whose whole family was trash?

There was one other thing I'd learned: It wasn't me who was trash—they were. They lied and covered up and gave bribes and polluted the river so you couldn't swim in it or eat the fish out of it. I wasn't trash—they were. I would never forget that lesson.

"Harry," Helen said. "Do you feel all right?"

"I'm all right," I said.

"Do you feel like eating?" she said. "I'm going to make spaghetti and meat sauce."

"It's nice to have Helen around again, isn't it, Harry?" Mom said.

JAMES LINCOLN COLLIER is the coauthor with his brother, Christopher Collier, of the Newbery Honor Book *My Brother Sam Is Dead*, *The Bloody Country*, *The Winter Hero*, *Jump Ship to Freedom*, *War Comes to Willy Freeman*, and *Who Is Carrie?* He has written many other highly acclaimed books for young readers, and for adults, including *The Making of Jazz: A Comprehensive History* and *Louis Armstrong: An American Genius*. He lives in New York City.